St. Ita:

The Forgotten Princess

(VITA SANTAE YTAE)

by

James Dunphy

Order this book online at www.trafford.com
or email orders@trafford.com

Most Trafford titles are also available at major online book retailers.

© Copyright 2006 James Dunphy.
All rights reserved. No part of this publication may be reproduced, stored in a
retrieval system, or transmitted, in any form or by any means, electronic, mechanical,
photocopying, recording, or otherwise, without the written prior permission of the author.

Print information available on the last page.

ISBN: 978-1-4120-7778-1 (sc)

Because of the dynamic nature of the Internet, any web addresses or links contained in
this book may have changed since publication and may no longer be valid. The views
expressed in this work are solely those of the author and do not necessarily reflect the
views of the publisher, and the publisher hereby disclaims any responsibility for them.

Any people depicted in stock imagery provided by Getty Images are models, and such
images are being used for illustrative purposes only.
Certain stock imagery © Getty Images.

Trafford rev. 06/26/2018

www.trafford.com

North America & international
toll-free: 844-688-6899 (USA & Canada)
fax: 812 355 4082

MUNSTER

Corcomroe
Inchiquin
Ibrickan
Tullagh
Arra
Upp. Ormond

Islands
Corcanderlagh
Kildysart
Owny
Kilnelongy

Moylarta

Iraghticonor
L I M E R
Clonnello
Clon William

Mc Clanmoris
U
N
S
Coshlea
Iffa

Trughenackmy
C
O
Duhallow
Armoy
Clongibbon
Collmor
W.A.

Maguinihie
Millstreet
Kilcrohy
Fermoy
Barrimore
Kilpatlow

Glanarooghty
C
O
C O U N

Mus
kery
Killeagh

Bantry
Kinsale

Carbury

Introduction

I was prompted to write this book to fulfil a commitment I made several years ago. Shortly before, I was assembling a collage of pictures representing significant people and events in the community and one of the contributions I was given was a picture of St. Ita, a figure with whom I had not been familiar before, despite the fact that several locations near me were named for her. I put this picture in the centre of the collection and became fascinated by the person it represented.

As a result of a conversation I had with a journalist from a local newspaper, he came to view the picture and was sufficiently impressed to suggest that I write a book on the local history of the area.

A year or so afterwards, I began to write the book and, by chance, again came across the picture of Ita. Now, she was not just the centre of the picture, but also a constant part of my consciousness.

For reasons which I cannot really recall, I made a promise to her that I would make her and her works known. I had no idea at that time just how extensive her travels had been, the effect she had on the community at the time, her miracles or her battles with the Druids.

When my dearest friend became ill and looked like he would not recover, I began praying to St. Ita. In the event, he died a short time later and some time afterwards, I experienced a vision of him walking towards a mansion and a woman of about fifty years, of strong build and whose face I did not see, emerge from the mansion and move towards him.

I have this picture of him turning away from us, as if he were leaving the cares of the world behind. He walked side by side with the mysterious woman into the mansion and I then realised that he was going to that better world which we know awaits those who believe it exists and desire and work to be there. I now have no doubt that this woman was St. Ita, who had contributed so much to our area and to the Munster counties particularly, when she lived here fifteen hundred years ago. I also believe that I have received regular guidance from her with this venture.

I then decided to research all I could find about the forgotten Saint, the Warrior Princess, the Holy Woman who inspired many others to follow her in the Christian Faith.

What follows is a summary of my search and research and is based on extracts from books and histories; from conversations with people of like mind in the various areas where St. Ita and her sister Eannaigh ministered to the people and from inspiration I received during the last few years.

I am not suggesting to anyone that this is all proven fact, but I offer it to those of an open mind as a representation of the life St. Ita led and her work to promote Christianity in Ireland shortly after St. Declan and St. Patrick introduced this new faith to this country.

I hope the reader will enjoy the book and gain some value and inspiration from it.

James Dunphy
October 2005

Foreword

Many miracles of extraordinary character are attributed to the Holy Virgin Ita, such as the restoration of sick and infirm persons to health and strength and even raising, on several occasions, the dead to life. She is said to have had a knowledge of transgressions which were thought to have been secret, known only to God, because from infancy she was accustomed to meditating on Divine things. She had been favoured with supernatural powers and if these were lacking in chronicles, the chroniclers paid the penalty of seeing their books cast aside as stale and unprofitable. It is this love of the sensational which is popular among simple souls. The real truthful record of martyr's ordeals survived through manuscripts. We cannot say whether these stories, which have either been destroyed or embellished, are true or not. Little is known or written about Ita through Munster, but yet, it is known she travelled the counties of the province as there are many stories about her handed down in folklore through generations, especially in places called Kilmeady, Killeedy and Kilmeaden, places all named for her as well as others besides. She travelled like Joan of Arc, fighting the Druids and freeing poor people from slavery.

Anything in the nature of stories connected to the life of Ita and the miracles worked through her, were not written for one to four centuries after her death. Somewhere along the way, her journeys through Munster must have been lost. Yet the folklore lived on. Not only was she known as Mary of Munster, as it was said she fostered the child Jesus, but she is also known as the Brigid of Munster and the White Sun of Munster. Another name by which she is known is the Mother of Vocations, as she sent priests and missionaries all over the world, to bring faith and the word of God to many. Elsewhere, among her many titles, Ita is called the Bright Sun of Munster. In looking at any documentation about her, it is necessary to apply the caution deserving of all medieval manuscripts.

The Travels of St. Ita

Ita was born on 1st May 476 and was named Deirdre, which was later changed to Ita.

490 AD	At age 14 she left Kilmeaden for Kill
490 AD	5 years in Kill
495 AD	8 Months in Kilmacthomas
495 AD	5 years in Clashmore
500 AD	4 months in Cork
501 AD	4 years in Killeedy Crossbarry
505 AD	5 years in Kilmeady Millstreet
510 AD	Ita was 34 when she reached Killeedy in Limerick

After some years in Killeedy, St. Ita went on her missions around Munster. After many years of travelling in the various counties of Munster and having crossed the Shannon into Clare, Ita spent the last fifteen years of her life in Killeedy. At this stage, she had become too old to travel.

St. Ita was about 80 years old when she died.

A Princess is Born

On the banks of the Suir in Kilmeadan, Co. Waterford, about the year 476 AD a girl who was named Deirdre, later to be known as Ita was born. An ancestor of hers called Hermon had been King of Tara in 580BC. During his reign, a ship of the Tribe of David, an adventurous tribe, was lost off what is now Carickfergus, on the north coast of Ireland. On board were a Princess named Tea Zephio, daughter of King Zedikian with her great-grandfather and guardian, a Prophet named Germiah. The Princess was said to have been the fairest maiden ever seen in Ireland.

Germiah was God's trustee of the blood line and the Throne of David. As they camped in a small grove, the mighty King Hermon and his warriors came by, returning from battle. The King was overawed by the beauty of the Princess and he sent a message ahead for his chariot to be brought.

The group from over the sea was taken to the palace and treated royally. The Princess and King Hermon became constant companions and soon, Hermon approached Germiah for permission to marry the Princess. He was successful and Princess Tea Zephio became Queen of Ireland and the happy couple reigned for many years. She was loved throughout the land and the Bards sang songs of her beauty and her smile.

Now, centuries later, the family, having lost the High Kingship, were led south by their Chieftain, Aengus the Intolerable and in this new land by the Suir, they carved out for themselves a new kingdom that reached from Cashel, southwards to the coast and ran from East to West along the valley of the Blackwater.

This conquest took place in the Third Century and within another hundred years, these terrible Decies had, with the baptism of Declan, son of the reigning Chief, shown the rest of Ireland that they had adopted and were organising the new faith. In the mid-Fifth Century, Patrick completed what Declan had begun and on the accession of young Gael MacCormick, the Decies had their first Christian king.

King Kennfoelad, Ita's father and King of the Upper Decies was a Christian and had married Necta, a Princess of the same faith, on the banks of the Suir in Kilmeadan, where Kennefoelad held court with Necta. It was a custom of that time that story-tellers and their listeners sat around open fires telling tales of how battles had been won and lost, what trophies and booty had been taken and how they had enriched both themselves and their reputations at the expense of their enemies.

In early spring, a royal, gifted child was born. Her father may have longed for a son, but the couple accepted their beautiful daughter to whom they gave the old Celtic name, Deirdre. But 'Deirdre of the Sorrows' was not to remain her name, as she was later nicknamed Ita, which can be interpreted as 'Thirst of God'. It is a mystery how, or by whom she was called Ita. Many parents today have named their new-born daughters Ita, especially those born around mid-January.

Site of St. Ita's Fort in Kilmeadan

In her early years, Ita's beauty became known throughout the land and, it is said, she was one of the most graceful and beautiful maidens to be found in Munster. The three lights that shone from her made her beauty seem unreal. The Bards and poets sang her praises.

Ita had many suitors calling to the banks of the Suir displaying their skills, trying to win her hand. A powerful prince Lóe Ghuire, son of Ui Niall came to Ita's father asking for her hand in marriage. The King was very pleased and thought he would be a suitable husband for Ita and also a strong ally for himself and his people. Ita would not accept the proposal and was adamant in her refusal. The prince was furious and did not realise that Ita was a baptised Christian and that his rival as her life-long companion was Jesus.

King Kennfoelad, fearing for the safety of his beautiful princess, sent her to a nearby wooded hill. Ita was unaware where this journey was leading to. The coachman stopped at the hill, which has since been known as Kilbarrymeadan - Cill Barra Méidín, Church of My Little Ita's Height. There, her craftsmen built her a chapel of wattle and thatch and, as Ita became known, people flocked to hear the good news of the Living God. Ita was a very prayerful person and often needed privacy and solitude, so the people built her an oratory at the bottom of the hill. This became known as Kilbeg (Cill Beag, the Little Chapel).

The site of St. Ita's Church at Kilbarrymeadan.

At the eastern side of the church ruin of Kilbarrymeadan is a remarkable holy well. The people call it St. Ita's Well (Tobar Barra

- 9 -

St. Ita's Church site near the site of the Fort at
Kilbeg, Kilbarrymeadan , Co. Waterford.

Méidín). This well is circular, fifteen feet in diameter and four feet in depth. It has been a place of veneration down through the ages to the present day. There are rags and tokens on the surrounding bushes, placed there as an indication of the strong faith and healing powers of St. Ita. There is no record kept of these people or where they come from.

ITA'S WELL KILBEG

Ita was known all along the coast from Bonmahon to Tramore and was loved by the fishermen who often felt inspired by her. In return, they named a little strand after her, Tráigh Máde Óig - 'Ita, the Virgin Strand' which is located near Boatstrand.

She told them many stories and we can imagine their great interest in the miracle of the loaves and the fishes. It was a story close to their own hearts and to their way of life. They too had spent many long days and nights on stormy waters and had caught nothing.

Ita fostered the story of Íosagán, the little Jesus and also many of the Holy People and Missionaries. Of all the saints, it is said that St. Brendan was her favourite. Their partings always caused great pain.

In today's world, where there is such a decline in vocations and a great need within the Church, we should be calling on Ita as the foster mother of the religious to inspire labourers into the harvest. While she was in Kilbarrymeadan, Ita was called by Jesus to go and learn about the sea and boats, for she would need that knowledge to be of assistance to Brendan to build his boats.

She was sought all over Munster for her advice, both by her holy followers and warring clans who had been fighting for years. She became known as the wise and holy judge, for whatever settlement was made, was accepted by the disputing parties. When a disagreement was particularly serious and her intervention was needed urgently, she often travelled overnight on her great white horse, protected by eight men.

A colourful and tasteful window in St. Brendan's Cathedral in Loughrea shows a gentle, stately Ita with the baby Brendan and an angel playing at her feet. A beautiful legend claims that the Infant Jesus appeared to Ita and an old Irish poem attributed to her, is a lullaby which she sang for Jesukin, her name for the Divine Child. Two translations of this poem are given in 'Hoggland, A Thousand Years of Irish Poetry'.

St.Ita's School,
Loughrea,
Co. Galway.

Confidence in Ita's intercession was unbounded and places as far as Cornwall dedicated churches and chapels to her. Ancient Litanies among spiritual communities on the Continent invoked her name and it also appears in Alcuin's poem on the Irish Saints.

In Killeedy, there is a well and also the ruins of a Romanesque church which, even today, is frequently decorated with flowers. A few miles away in Boolaveeda - St. Ita's Milking Place - there is an ancient enclosure.

St Ita's Well is in the graveyard in Killeedy. The well is 18 inches in diameter and 3 feet in depth. When we visited it, the well was dry, but there is water in the well at different times of the year. The rounds are made on January 15th and the well is believed to cure smallpox. Flowers often surround the well. Legend has it that St Ita asked for a drink here and was given lukewarm water. She threw this water on the ground and a well sprung up. It is said that you cannot boil the water.

(From Limerick Diocesan Website:
www.limerickdioceseheritage.org/Killeedy)

St Ita's Monastery site Killeedy, Limerick

St Ita's Church Killeedy, Limerick

St Ita's Church, Ashford, Limerick

Some of Ita's chapels were roofed with stone, while others were thatched. All were of simple origin, about six or seven feet high, mostly with mud walls but some were built of stone. The walls were white-washed both inside and out and they usually had

Statue of St Ita in Killeedy Parish Church, Limerick

two windows and one door in the centre of the west gable. The floor was made of packed clay and the typical altar was in the west wing and made of stone or timber.

Statue of the Blessed Virgin Mary, St Michael's Limerick.

These chapels had no porch, sacristy or churchyard; no interior decorations and only a crucifix behind the altar. There is no reference to statues or stations of the cross from the period and there were no seats, with people having to stand or sit on the floor. Some old people brought woven súgán pads made from long grass on which to kneel. Others brought slates to kneel on as a method of punishment.

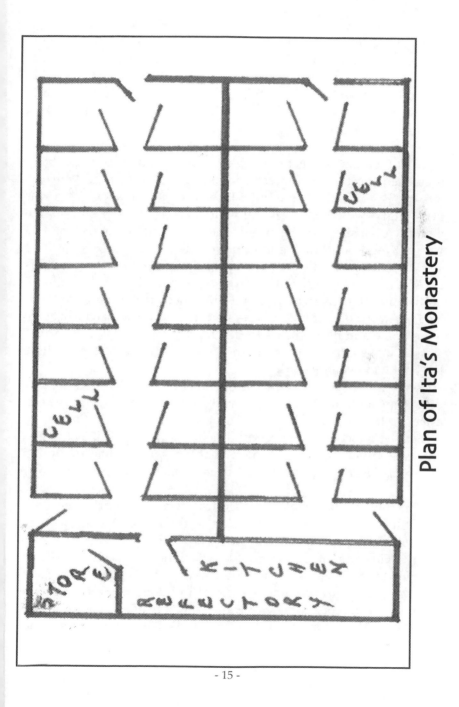

Plan of Ita's Monastery

Many stories have been told about Ita as a child on the Banks of the Suir in Kilmeaden and it appears she spent a lot of time by that river. In the mornings she would gaze into the Suir and on seeing her reflection would fix a smile on her face, a smile that would remain on her countenance throughout the day, no matter what trouble or trying moments came her way.

One day, when the little Princess was very young, she went to the river and managed to get into a boat. She shoved off from the bank unnoticed and there was great uproar and confusion when she was missed. Her minders were brought before Queen Necta, who was very angry with them. Like any mother she was frantic at the thought of losing her beautiful daughter and, to make matters worse, King Kennfoelad and his men were out of camp.

Where was the little Princess and the missing boat, the searchers asked themselves fruitlessly? Dark was setting in and she still had not been found. Everybody slowly returned to the camp, sad and weary. A wise old Holy Man was sent for and he advised everyone to go home and rest in peace for the night.

God looks after his own, he said and he blessed the spot where the boat had been moored.

People rose early next morning feeling heavy-hearted and, as they were about to restart their search, they spotted the boat. There, asleep at the stern was the child Ita.

Praise for God was on everybody's lips and, even as they hugged and chided her, her parents knew that that journey had brought a big change in Ita. Where she had been, what she had seen, nobody knew.

Sometimes when the young Princess wanted to be alone with God, she would cross the River Suir to the Hill of Mona Vie. One day somebody reported that the hill was on fire and, fearful for Ita's safety, King Kennfoelad sent his warriors to rescue her. They manned the boats quickly and when they got to the other side, there was the young girl kneeling, suspended mid-air above the ground praying. Instead of a fire, there was a heavenly glow all around her. They returned and informed the King and Queen of what they had seen and they knew that this too had to do with the earlier disappearance of Ita and the changes they saw in her on her return.

St. Ita's Hill at Mona Vie, Co. Kilkenny.

It was Eastertime, one year from the close of the fifth century, Kennfoelad's household had celebrated the feast of the Resurrection with music and banqueting, welcoming after the long winter months, the eggs and butter brought in by the dairy maids.

Ita, then a girl of about fourteen, stood with her sister Eannaigh watching a cumhal as she churned. "Your mother wants you to take some butter to Dara, the widow woman that lives by Fintan's chapel," said the woman. "I will give you a drop of milk along with it. Dara has only one cow and itís as lean as herself." She sliced off a piece of butter as she spoke and wrapped it in a few leaves.

Ita and the younger child took the jug and ran across the fields to Dara's hut, which was one of the beehive dwellings common at the time, and which seemed dark to the children coming in from the sunshine. They had not known that Dara's son was ill and so they were unprepared when the widow whom they now saw crouching by the smoking fire, cried out: "My child is dying. Why have you come to this house of sorrow?"

Statue in St Ita's Church, Ashford Limerick

Statue of St. Ita in St. Michael's Church Limerick

Was it not enough, thought the woman bitterly, that she should have to sit in this hovel and watch her son die, without being asked to contrast him with the smiling, well-fed children of the rich?

Eannaigh, who had been looking forward to seeing the womanís surprise at the presents they had brought her, began to cry, but the older girl had an intuition of what the woman was suffering. She crossed the room and sat down beside her, close to where the four year old boy was lying on a pile of straw.

"Tell me about your son Colman," she said, "maybe we could get something that would help him."

"It began two days ago," said the woman "and the pain seems to be in his head. He holds it stiffly all the time, and he's been saying strange words and not knowing me or his sister."

They both looked at the child.

"Colman," said Ita, "do you not know your mother?" He did not reply, and the restless eyes focused on neither of them. Dara turned suddenly to the girl beside her.

"Pray for him," she urged, "you've never sinned as I have sinned; pray for him, they're telling me he has a devil."

Paganism was still rife in the country, and with it the ugly fear that victims of meningitis were possessed. Ita, frightened by the woman's wild words, began to pray, while the younger child moved so close to her sister that she was touching her. Dara, who had tried to pray, found she could only repeat one word over and over. "God" she kept saying, "God".

Meanwhile, Ita had hidden her face in her hands. "Holy Trinity," said the child, "Holy Trinity, Father, Son and Holy Spirit." She tried to see them living in her soul, three bright jewels, they seemed to her, merging in one aura of light, "Father, Son and Holy Spirit, King of the bright Heavens, You have the power to give life and health, You have the power, You have the power."

When, after many moments she opened her eyes, she was hardly surprised to see Colman's gaze resting steadily on her. He was still tired, but his head now rested naturally on his pillow of straw.

"Is he going to get better," asked Eannaigh staring at him.

"Yes," said Ita, "yes, thank God."

The peasant woman said nothing at first, because she was crying with joy, but she followed the children to the door where, half-hysterically, she called after Ita.

"May the Son of the Virgin gather you into His arms. May He hold you there forever, and may you be the Blessed Mother of many children. "

"What happened?" Eannaigh kept asking on the way home. "Why did the little boy get better so quickly?"

"Because we asked God to cure him," she answered. "God can do anything He likes." To her it was as simple as that.

*　　　　*　　　　*　　　　*　　　　*

Queen Necta was sitting with her daughters and their nurse in her grianán, a smooth lawn in the sunniest part of the rath. Necta was still a young woman, fair like Ita, but gentler and dreamier, finding in her new religion the happiness she had not found in her marriage with Kennfoelad. Fintan, an old Holy Man who lived nearby, was her confessor and anam chara - the "soul friend" who guided her through the years of her married life. It was he who had given Ita her name, changing it from Deirdre which had been her father's choice.

"Why would you give her a pagan name?" he had asked Kennfoelad in a tone few would have used with that potentate. "Can you not see the thirst for God in that child's eyes?" And to their surprise, Necta remembered, Kennfoelad had given in, calling the girl Ita, a name which signifies thirst, or desire for God.

Now as the women and girls embroidered, Necta recited to them from some of the old sagas, for she was a cultured woman who loved the poetry and legend of her race. "What shall I tell you now?" she asked after a few minutes silence. "Would you like a story about the sailors who fetch our Mass wine from the south, or one about the great Abbot of Rome who lives in the palace that the King of the world gave to him."

When they asked to be told of Ercnat, the Queen went on, half singing the familiar words.

"There was once a king called Daire," she began, "great grandson of Niall of the Nine Hostages. Daire was ruling over Armagh at the time that Patrick went there to ask for land on which to build a church. Patrick was given the land, and when his new church was completed, he invited the King to attend Mass there with his family. During Mass, princess Ercnat, the King's pagan daughter, grew so entranced by the singing of a young cleric named Benen, that she fell in love with him. But Benen, because he was a monk, would not return her love."

"And did she mind?" asked Eannaigh, looking intently into the Queen's face, and hoping that the story would somehow have a happy ending.

"Oh, yes," said Necta, looking in return at the child, and wondering how long she would remain detached from passion and untroubled by human love. "Yes, she felt a sorrow so great that it nearly caused her death."

"Served her right, the bold creature," said the nurse, breaking a thread with her teeth.

"And then," continued the Queen, "Daire told Patrick the whole story, and begged him to pray for his daughter. Patrick was so touched by what he heard that he ordered Benen to go to the dying girl, and sprinkle her with holy water. The young monk obeyed, and his prayers with those of Patrick, restored Ercnat to life, but the true miracle was that when Ercnat awoke, her heart was free once more. Going to Patrick she made a vow of virginity, and received from his hands a white veil. From then on she spent her life in prayer and in making vestments for the church at Armagh, and never again was her heart troubled with love for mortal man."

"How beautiful," said Eannaigh, but Ita said nothing; she had seemed scarcely to listen. Her mother looked at her intently. Lately she had found her elder daughter more difficult to understand. Perhaps, she thought, she was growing too old for these tales. A sense of loneliness came over her, but she was too proud to ask her child for her confidence.

"We're making vestments, too," said Eannaigh still thinking of Ercnat.

"We've a great many other things to make besides vestments,î said the nurse, ìthink of all the cloaks and tunics you will need for your trousseau. That girl is thirteen now," she added, pointing her needle at Ita, ìand it will be no time at all before her father has her married off."

"She can marry if she wants to," said Eannaigh "but I'm like Cruimtheris, the Lombard princess, who lived alone with a doe to give her milk, and her own little apple tree to give her fruit."

"You might find it lonely," said her mother, but here at least, she had a child who needed her.

"But you would visit me," Eannaigh told her.

Suddenly, Ita smiled and the others laughed too. The young queen wished it could be like this always, the three of them in their grianán away from the drinking and coarse talk she so often had to witness in her husband's banqueting hall; away from the scheming and jealousy that bred civil war. But what her cumhal had said was true, her oldest child was nearing womanhood, and Kennfoelad, careless of her happiness, would marry her to whichever ally he most favoured, or whichever enemy he most feared.

*   *   *   *   *

It was nearing Bealtaine of the following year. Ita and Eannaigh were walking through the woods where their father hunted, when

- 21 -

the cracking of twigs and the voices of men told them that some riders were approaching. The girls turned and saw a party of huntsmen coming towards them, led by a young man who was evidently their chief. He reined in his horse and asked Ita whose territory he had entered. She told him. The nobleman thanked her, then having asked her name, rode away with his friends. But as the chieftain rode on he noticed an apple tree in flower and wondered that it should remind him of Ita.

Some weeks later, Queen Necta and her daughters were sitting again in their grianán with the grass about them daisy white, just as they had done on so many summer days. A chariot approached the rath and Eannaigh went to see who was in it. She stood near the gate, and saw that her father had already gone forward to meet the young nobleman whose arrival she had heard.

He was taller than Kennfoelad, the child noticed, and was dressed like the son of a king. Her gaze wandered to his chariot, and to the horses which a boy was holding with difficulty. This was Loe Ghuire, Prince of Leinster and heir to the throne.

Meanwhile Kennfoelad and his guest had been conversing, and now Eannaigh's sharp eyes saw that the older man was afraid of the other. The two men noticed Eannaigh, and before she had time to disappear her father called her over.

"My younger daughter," he said, introducing her. Eannaigh looked up at her father with questioning, unfriendly eyes, then turned to the stranger and recognised him.

"We met you in the woods last month," she said shyly.

"That's right, little girl," he replied.

"Eannaigh," said Kennfoelad with awkward kindness, "ask your mother to have a meal prepared immediately. Tell her that we have a royal guest."

"Not more royal than you," the young man protested, as Kennfoelad, his right arm around the boy's shoulder, led him to the banqueting hall, a smile of triumph lighting up his strong, red face.

The child ran back to the grianán and when her mother had left them, she tried to tell her sister all that she had seen. "It's the hunter we met in the woods before Bealtaine," she said, "he wears a great cloak with a hem of red gold, and a brooch of woven gold to hold it. There is every bright colour on the léine he wears; even the horses that draw his chariot have their manes dyed bright as the red of a yewberry.

"I do not know his name," said Eannaigh, "but he can be no less than a king or the son of a king."

Meanwhile within the great wooden banqueting hall the two men were talking together.

"I have heard much about your daughter," the younger man was saying, "and I am convinced that the love I bear her is a love not unworthy of my rank. O, King, I see her as a second Emer, holding in her hands the six gifts of womanhood. Give me your child, Kennfoelad, son of Cormac, let her be queen of my lands." He grew silent then, but his eyes still shone.

Middle-aged and cynical, Kennfoelad listened uncomfortably. He did not want this young idealist, this would-be Cuchulain, to suspect that he was only too glad to give him the girl, and when he did reply there was some sincerity in his words. "You'll make her happy," he said, "why should I refuse you?"

"Then she's mine?"

"She is yours," replied Kennfoelad.

The Queen was sent for and asked to bring the Princess Ita to her father. They waited, then she came towards them, a tall young girl, the sun behind her lighting up her hair.

"I think your mother has explained why we've asked you to come to us," said Kennfoelad, but he spoke too loudly and too cheerfully.

"Yes, Father".

"And what reply do you wish to make?"

Ita hesitated and stayed silent for a few moments. Then she emphatically said "Father I will not marry this Royal Prince or any other man."

Both men looked at her in amazement. King Kennfoelad became very angry as he was getting on in years and wanted a young man to fight his battles. He knew he could never reconcile the Prince even if his daughter was to change her mind, which he knew she would not.

Still he was determined to terminate all her godly thoughts. Why could not that man Patrick have stayed in his own country and let those Celtic kings rule as they always had.

When Ita refused the Prince he became ferocious and threatened her father with war. Loe Ghuire, the mighty warrior from Tara expected to take over from Kennfoelad and at the same time add to his own territory and enlarge his own kingdom by uniting the lands of Munster and Leinster. It is not difficult to imagine his anger when he discovered that his dream would never come to pass. Loe Ghuire was a handsome young man, who could have chosen any young woman he wished to be his bride, but he did not realise that Ita was a baptized Christian and that he was competing with the Heavenly Prince, Jesus.

With rage, Loe Ghuire, son of Ui Niall ordered his horse to be brought quickly and, with his men, rode away in fury and crossed the river Suir into Leinster.

Kennfoelad ordered two horses to be saddled, one for himself and one for his friend Conla, who was one of the most influential nobles of the Decies. They rode with their horses through the countryside along the banks of the Suir. No words were exchanged as they journeyed in silence. Conla had never before seen his friend in this strange mood. They continued on through Cashel and right around for the coast of Youghal and Ardmore. Conla had fought many battles accompanied by his friend. On their return home they travelled for days without stopping for food or sleep.

When they crossed the Mahon they came to a beautiful peaceful wood on a hill. There they stopped and the king raised his hand and they dismounted. Conla lit a fire and went in search of food. Kennfoelad still remained silent and with his saddle for a pillow, lay down and fell fast asleep. At first he twisted and turned as if troubled and showed signs of extreme anguish. Then a calm came over him and he slept peacefully. He was watched closely at all times by his dear friend. There, the king in his sleep had visions of his daughter standing at the gates of heaven. Three spirits, looking like kings, came to meet her. She was dressed like a great Celtic warrior. Suddenly Kennfoelad was awake and his first words to his friend were "I must get back to the Suir". Then he opened his heart to his friend and told him of his frustrations, from the day Ita was born. His plans for her included her marriage to the great prince Loe Guire who had asked for her hand. Her refusal was a great surprise and so, instead of an ally he'd have an enemy. Even the king could now see Ita in a different light and like everybody else knew that God had His own special plan in store for this wonderful girl. "We must hurry back," he said, "I know my daughter is in danger."

Kennfoelad, sensing his daughter's danger ordered her to leave immediately for a nearby wooded hill. He told her mother to accompany Ita but the Queen refused. She knew the King was in danger and as she was closer to him now than they had been for a long time, she remained by his side.

Ita packed her trunk. Tearfully she bid farewell to her loved ones and all those who had helped her in her fourteen young years. She blessed herself in Latin, Greek and Irish. Those who witnessed this blessing saw a beautiful light hovering around her. They also blessed themselves feeling that they too were in the presence of God.

Ita entered the waiting carriage without a backward glance and even as she settled herself and the carriage moved off, she knew she would never again set foot in what had been her home for fourteen years. She would always have the happy memories of her childhood days and the games she played, some of which she had won and others she had lost like any normal child.

Ita was accompanied on her journey by some young girls, an older woman, servants and soldiers. She passed through the courtyard, by the beehive buildings and the houses along the Suir she loved so well.

The last building was the little church. Leaving it behind her, receding into the distance was a cause of great pain to her as she remembered the happy times she had spent there with the Virgin son. It was here that God gave her the three previous jewels that would light up her life forever. The picture of this little church with its Celtic windows and its special big window behind the altar, would always be vivid in her mind.

It was night-time, the roads were rough and they moved along at a steady pace. The horses seemed to pick their steps as if they knew where they were going.

They travelled through the townlands of Blacknock and Knockaderry and their orders were not to stop until they reached the wooded hill. Coming to the townland of Carrickphilip, their way was blocked by a number of fierce looking druids. They had torches with bands of light coming from them. It was weird and frightening and it dazzled men and horses.

"Halt," called one of their leaders, "where are you bound for, young lady?"

"We are going to the next hill to build a church, to bring the Word of the living God to His people," said Ita.

"Now, now," said the big man dressed in black, "your Gods are like figures on top of a hill, all fire and no power. If it is Gods you want, we can give them to you. They have the whole universe at their command." Now he spoke with a voice like thunder. "How dare you blaspheme our sacred gods. You will have to pay for this. We are your masters. It is we who determine where you go."

Ita ordered her men to draw their swords. The Kilmeaden men amounted to fourteen, the Druids clan consisted of twenty tall men with long and heavy swords. The battle began, forwards, backwards, shifting, eluding the swords that went up, down and horizontally, as the combatants swung at one another. The Kilmeaden men had the lesser numbers. The Druids and their lofty gods were getting the upper hand, as most of their opponents were out of the fight. Ita could see the triumph on the Druids' faces and her men becoming fatigued. The young princess knew something must be done. She prayed as she never prayed before. 'Come dear God in our hour of need. Come Jesus, we need You. Do not let us perish. Come Lord, come. These men are good; do not let them perish. Come Lord come, come'.

Now all of her men who had been on the ground wounded, suddenly rose and returned to the fight. Their swords took on a glow. They seemed to mow down the Druids, all of whom were paralysed, all but one young man who was left standing. He begged the girl for a truce. Their forces diminished, he went down on his knees saying 'Great and gentle Lady, forgive us for the wrong we have done. Ask your God not to be angry with us'. He asked to go back to his high priest who now looked ghastly and could barely speak, muttering 'Give the princess our greeting. We will not hinder her again. Ask her to ask her God to restore the injured men to their former health. One of them is my only son and I will be forever grateful. When the messenger returned, all of the fighting Druids were again on their feet, though looking dazed. The young messenger Druid asked if he could join her band and she agreed. The skirmish lasted six to eight hours and it was now approaching night time. The country was rough and wild, so it was decided to stay in the nearby rath called Caheruane, where they were made welcome. They continued their journey next morning, arriving in Kill on the wooded hill, now known as Kilbarrymeaden.

They formed a group to protect her. There were nine forts in a radius of two miles which protected Ita. There were three in Lissahane and one each in Caheruane, Ballineen, Ballymurrin, Rathquague, Ballyvadden and Ballyristeen.

She stayed in one of the outlying forts, one of the three at Lissahane and many people came to see her here, even from as far away as Newcastle, Portlaw and further afield.

When they reached the wooded hill, all appeared very quiet and peaceful. Itaís father, the King, often hunted there, so he would be quite familiar with the area. Ita made this secluded place her home for the next five years.

Henceforth, it was to be known as Kilbarrymeadan, Ita's Church on the Hill.

In return, the fishermen chose a little strand in Boatstrand to name after her; Tráigh Míde Óige - Ita the Virgin Strand. There, Ita fostered the memory and teaching of Íosagán.

Map showing the nine forts in a ring which
protected St. Ita when she was in the Kilbarrymeadan.

Ita's Evil Uncle

Some time after Princess Ita arrived in Kill, Loe Ghuire, the Mad Prince approached Ita's uncle in Coolfin, offering him gold and silver if he would go to Ita in Kilbarrymeadan and entice her to forget this Jesus whom she loved. Her uncle said he did not need either gold or silver, but had always wished for a small kingdom of his own. The Prince promised him a small part of Connaught, a promise he could hardly fulfil, as his power lay only in Leinster.

Her uncle, with five others, set out for Kilbarrymeadan on horseback and went straight to Princess Ita. He told her that the Mad Prince could make her one of the greatest ladies in all of Ireland and that she would be foolish to refuse his offer. He could have any woman he wished for, he said, but he had chosen Ita. He could give her riches and jewels and he pointed out to her how lucky she was to have such a great man's love. Why do you follow this God-man, Patrick, he asked, as he is a foreigner. It should be left to the kings of Ireland to decide whom Irish princesses should marry.

He thought to soft-talk her into coming away with him to meet with Loe Ghuire, but Ita told him she did not need or want any worldly things and that she was quite happy with her life as it was.

Her conniving uncle got very angry with her and began to shout at her. He could see his kingdom slipping away from him and he accused her of being evil and of following an evil god. He said she had put her evil eye on the great prince and he would now kill her father and all her people in revenge. He would take her as a slave, he threatened, and she should now consent to marriage before it was too late.

Her gods would not save her, he continued and the blood which would be spilt in Kilbarrymeadan would be neither his nor the Prince's, but that of her household.

Go, you foolish man, Ita told her scheming uncle, tell your prince he is wasting his valuable time as my only Prince is Jesus Christ. As he departed in fury, her uncle promised that she had not seen the last of the Prince, as he would come and take her anyway. He added that he would not now get his promised land because of her continued refusal to co-operate.

Her evil uncle and his party mounted their horses and rode away, planning to return and kidnap her another night. On the way home, near Ballynageeragh, Dunhill, they came into conflict with a party of twenty Druids who wanted to know what plans he had made to kidnap the young princess, saying they were prepared to give him money for the information.

Nothing could substitute for the land he would get from the Prince, however and he emphatically rejected the Druids' offer, telling his men to draw their swords. As it all happened quickly, only he and one of his men had time to arm themselves, before the strong force was upon them and soon, they both lay dying on the ground. Their bodies were then loaded on their horses and brought back and buried somewhere in Kilmeadan.

Boatstrand
Tráigh Míde Óg (Ita, the Virgin Strand)

Tra Míde Óg at Boatstrand

One night as she rested, Ita had a vision of Christ with a young man, showing him how to build a ship. He seemed to be asking for her help. Soon afterwards, she went to a place now known as Boatstrand and there she met an elderly man, experienced in ship building. She asked for his help and he taught her all that was needed to build and sail a ship.

She went to the sea shore twice a week and loved to go out to sea in the boats with the fishermen. She told them many parables especially those relating to Jesus and the fisherman Peter; how he was afraid to step out of the boat and walk over the water to Jesus. She told them of how Jesus said to the fishermen of his time to 'launch out into the deep water and let down your nets for a catch'. They answered Him saying, "Master, we have laboured all night and have caught nothing, nevertheless at Your word we will let down the nets. When they had done that, they enclosed a great amount of fish, so much that their nets were breaking. Then Jesus asked them to follow him and He would make them fishers of men".

Once, while talking to two fishermen on the shore, Ita called out suddenly. She had had a vision that out at sea, out of sight, she could see two of their fellow fishermen in danger of their boat being capsized. Neither of them could swim.

"Man the boats" she cried. They replied that the sea was too dangerous and they could not launch. Ita said: "I speak for God. You will be safe, have no fear." Ita and the two men went out to sea and they came upon the two fishermen just as their boat capsized, leaving them no hope but to drown. When they saw the lovely Princess they thought she must be an angel. Ita and the fishermen brought their companions home safely to land and the rescued men were deeply grateful to her for having saved their lives.

    *   *   *   *   *

On another occasion, a large boat carrying fifty druids got into trouble in a storm off the south east coast, near the beach which carries Ita's name. In the midst of rough waves and pounded by strong winds it was seen that the boat would be sunk. After a period in which the occupants tried to steer from the shore, the boat was finally dashed against the rocks. It seemed that all of its people would be lost. The fishermen looked on helplessly, for there was nothing they could do. Then the Princess Ita came on the shore and, seeing the terrible plight of those on board, beseeched Jesus to calm the waters.

Suddenly the sea grew calmer and the fishermen were quickly to the rescue. All thirty men, fifteen women and five children on board were saved. Four of the children had passed out and were carried ashore by the local men. Everyone present cried for joy at the miracle and the rescue and even as they gave thanks, the strong winds resumed. The boat was dashed against the rocks and broken into matchwood. These strange people were more than grateful and they were given food and shelter for two nights. Ita stayed with them until they were fit to resume their journey. Twenty five were going to Baile na Giorrai near Dunhill, Co. Waterford to augment the druid presence there and the other twenty five were going to Carrick on Suir, Co. Tipperary to bring their numbers up to strength too. They were grateful to Ita and the community which had rescued them and wondered about the great power which the stately woman could call on which could calm the very elements themselves.

The Battles of Kill and Dunhill

Word spread among the Druids of this powerful, beautiful, young princess, who, with her Gods, was capable of taking over Munster. It was foretold that this would happen as it had been seen in the stars. The Druids were worried and wondered how they could hinder her. A meeting was called to decide what measures they should take to carry out this plan. No half measures will work where this powerful girl is among us, they agreed. One of the clever Druids said she and her followers must be totally exterminated.

The whole fort would have to be wiped out and levelled to the ground, he maintained, just as a fire which has been completely extinguished cannot continue to burn. How can we do this with what little men we have, they wondered. Ita, known in the area as Princess Kennfoelad, had a large number of men, with the Gaels and other friends also helping her.

The Druids knew that they would need a great army to defeat her. The Chief Druid who had been sent from England to reorganise the Dunhill Druids, said that he had ambitions to erect many Druids' altars, but was faced with the problem of Ita on his arrival. He pledged he would not be beaten by a mere girl, whatever powers she may have. A messenger was sent to the head of the English Druids conveying to them the seriousness of the situation and requesting a large force to be sent to Dunhill.

The Druids' Altar in Dunhill

The Druids in England were in their darkest hour. They had been shattered by the revolt and the unrest it had caused. They began their punitive campaign which became a reign of terror over the surviving Celts. When asked for help from the Druids of Dunhill, they were only too eager to send a detachment of a large group of their fighting men to Ireland, saying they might regain their former greatness in Ireland which they had now lost in Britain. One hundred professional fighting men were sent to Dunhill. They all came together in one boat, fourteen rowing at each side. They landed in Boatstrand, berthed their boat and moved to Dunhill. They rested for a week and then called a meeting. They wanted all the information they could get as to how this maiden had developed so much power.

The Dunhill Druids recalled to the English Druids how she had saved them as they tried to land. Their boat was wrecked by a storm and smashed against the rocks. The young maiden calmed the angry sea and soon they were able to land safely. As soon as they were safe the storm began again. She took care of their injuries and watched over them through the night, right through to their journey's end.

How many fighters did this great woman have? Who was her commander - her father, his right hand man, a very shrewd nobleman, one of the ablest fighting men in the Decies? How many fighting men could she call upon? How could they be summoned? A smoke signal could be sent and they would arrive within an hour. All in all, they could muster two or three hundred strong fighting men.

It was agreed they would try a few skirmishes to see how quickly the Gaels could come to her aid. They attacked in this way on six different occasions in the space of ten days. They attacked at dawn, deciding that at eight o'clock in the morning, the smoke signal could not be seen and they could have Ita's fort and, more importantly to them, Ita herself, wiped out before she could get help.

About 150 men set out from Béal na Giorraí, a small number of them on horseback. They were armed with spears and swords, and with bows and arrows, which were mainly used to start fires in the enemy encampment. They headed up through Ballyleen, straight for the fort and along by the area known as "Coffey's Rock". These were strong men over six feet tall and weighing an average of fourteen or fifteen stone each.

That morning at 4 am, all was quiet and Ita heard her name being called. "Wake up my child, make haste, your enemy is at the gate. It is time to call in your people."

Ita woke her father and soon messengers were sent out on horseback to seek help. By 6 am, a force had been gathered together around Carrigeen. Conola and Kenfoelad had a battle plan drawn up. The men took their places. Seventy were detailed to defend the fort; one hundred and fifty were placed on the south easterly side, while the remainder defended the west side, leaving the gap to the north east.

The Druids rode straight to the fort unhindered and suddenly, as they arrived at their destination, men arose out of nowhere. The Druids were taken by surprise for a few moments. Then battle began between their forces and Princess Ita of Kill. The battle was fast and furious. The Druids moved forward to take possession of the fort, only to find themselves surrounded by a strong force of Gaels they thought they had avoided. The ring of steel could be heard as swords clashed in the morning light. It was attack and counter attack. Horses were killed and fell on their riders. The Druids, who were great fighters, thought they could still win the day. As they were superior swordsmen they were able to retreat to lower ground. What the Gaels lacked in fighting skill and ability, was made up for in their bravery and they had a great impact on the battle. A mere lad of sixteen with a ragged cloak acquitted himself nobly. Although wounded, he refused to withdraw from the battlefield.

Kennfoelad and his leading man, Conola urged the fighters on by word and deed. Battles had been previously won but, for the Gaelic warriors, this exceeded all others by far. The Druids, though heavily outnumbered, put up a great fight and several times had almost broken through the defences. The Gaels, outnumbered 2 to 1, always seemed to have a comrade to help him to defeat his foe. The heavy loss of men drained the Druids enthusiasm. After one last and fiercely gigantic struggle, the order was given to flee if they could, as their lines had become broken and disordered. The Gaelic force relentlessly pursued them until finally the Druids accepted defeat.

Now Princess Ita moved on to the battlefield, thanking God for victory, a gentle young maiden, full of compassion for the wounded. She ensured that quarter was shown to those who looked for it and that the wounded of the losing side were carried to the fort to receive attention and humane treatment. One of the leaders of the Druids who was nearly seven feet tall and seventeen stone in weight, had to be carried away.

In previous battles, Britons with such great injuries would be left to die on the battlefield. Now, there was amazement in the eyes of the Druids, their gaze deepening in wonderment. Those English Druids were now ready to worship the ground Ita walked on, so deep was the impression she made with her beauty and gentle treatment.

The following morning, before they left the fort to make their journey back, the leader offered Ita his sword, saying her power was great, as was the power of her God. He declared that he now abandoned the God he had worshipped, and decided the true living God would be the one he would follow from now on. He asked Ita to come to Baile na Giorraì, Dunhill to baptise the rest of his followers. She bid them all a fond farewell and returned to the house of prayer with her commander, thanking God for His help.

Within two days, she went to Baile na Giorraí with five men, including King Kenfoelad and Conola. A great welcome awaited her. All kinds of coloured cloths and flags were hanging on poles to celebrate the occasion. The party went to the Druids own well to be baptised and it resembled the baptism in the Jordan. The leader of the English Druids became a Christian leader, a devout holy man. He ordered his followers to build a church for God and for Ita. It was built in Shanaclune and, with the blessing of the local chief, Ita baptised the Gaels shortly after.

From then on, the Gaels and the Druids became a single united force and even to this day this feeling of a united community is evident in the people of the area.

Cappagh, Dunhill

Cappagh, now known as Shanaclune, is situated near the village of Dunhill. There is an old church site in the farmyard of the late Michael (Mick) Murphy. His son Eamonn is able to point out where the site of the Penal church stood. He can remember a time when his father dug foundations for a new building and human bones were excavated which were reburied farther out. He says that if the ground was either all wet or all dry, those bones would last for all time. On the other hand, if the ground alternated in those conditions, those bones would deteriorate in a short time.

Several centuries ago, there stood a kitchen-sized inn just above south east. It was called Seán Pad's, where men played cards to a limit of a half-penny a game, a sum which at that time would buy a good dinner for a man. Only the very well off could afford to play and it was an honour for the younger ones to be allowed to watch. When the clergy, who were still being hunted at the time, suddenly appeared, the game would stop. Mass was celebrated in the humble abode, but the holy priest could not delay too long.

St. Ita's Well at Dunhill, where the Druids were baptised.

Shanaclune, where the Druids built a Church for St. Ita

There is a graveyard there which appears to have been unusually large for those penal times. The Druid settlement of more than a thousand years before seems to account for that.

The leader of Druids who had been baptised by Ita, came to believe in the true and living God, forsaking all other false gods. In time, he became a very holy man and led his people to be true and loyal Christians, making a strong bond between themselves and local Gaels, which even today makes them a strong united people. To show his gratitude to Ita, he had his craftsmen build a church in her honour. It was built on the right side of the entrance to what is now the Murphy homestead, on the brow of the hill, about thirty yards from the road fence. The church measured ninety feet by sixty feet and was in use up to the 7th century, lasting for a hundred and forty years.

Alone with God

One evening, as Ita returned from the seashore with some fish which the boatmen had given her. She spoke to them about the Lord God and how they should do His bidding and keep His commandments to gain their eternal reward. She went to pray in the oratory the local men had built for her, just twenty-five yards from her holy well in Kilbeg.

She prayed fervently for guidance and asked Jesus to steer her through a single life and to obey him in all things. She bowed her head and she felt alone and confused as she prayed. "My God, my God, I feel so alone," she prayed aloud and after, she felt a great presence with her. A lovely soft, deep voice spoke to her. "Lift up your head, my dear child," the voice said and when she raised her head, there stood Jesus. She blinked her eyes as a great peace came over her. The figure in front of her wore a blue cloak and underneath was a dress-like garment of yellow colour, much softer than the harsh colour we now know as gold.

There was a broad band around his waist which shone as if it were a light. It was the colour of silver. Again the figure before her spoke in that soft, deep voice saying: "God is well pleased with you my young girl; you have won many souls for God. You have won great battles and have shown great mercy and kindness. You will have to move away from those people you have grown to love. God asks this from people who love him. Go away from your kindred, your father's house and your country and I will make you the mother of a great people. You will bring good news to the poor and I will make you the light of a great nation. Do not be afraid, my child, as I am your protector in all your trials. It is the Lord who speaks."

Ita blinked her eyes and He was gone. Again, for a few moments, she felt alone, but as she rubbed her eyes once more, she felt a great strength come to her and she sat there for a long time. She then went out among her people, administering to their needs once again.

Ita's Spirituality

Much of Ita's worship took place out of doors, in groves, forests, clearings, at wells and on many mountain pilgrimages. This emphasises the nearness of God to us. Involvement in nature and everyday life cultivates intimacy with God who is nearer to us than ourselves. Ita had a prayer for everything; rising in the morning, going to bed at night, a prayer for rain, wind and sun. She had a special prayer when milking the cows or when a new animal was born. Evidence of Ita's spirituality and prayerful life can be seen in all she did and said.

Kilbarrymeadan

When Ita was about sixteen years old, she caused a church to be built on the Hill of Malacaun, measuring fifty feet by twenty, for the people at Kilbarrymeadan. The faithful came from a wide area to worship and the church was always full for their celebrations. The people had learned a great deal from her, such as better ways of living, better ways to farm, cook, but most of all, a better knowledge of the one, true God to whom they gave their allegiance.

She took the poor away from the Druids and with Dunhill also in the hand of God under the former Druid in whom she had full confidence, she was happy. She was aware that God could move her any time, so she made a visit to Boatstrand, which was to be her last. She knew that the Lord had a great deal more work for her to do and, as His servant, she asked for His guidance. She appointed three holy men, one of them a fisherman, to take care of the church. She instructed the three and then blessed them and felt satisfied that she was ready to go at anytime.

Kilmacthomas / Rossmede
Kilnagrange / Rathmeadan

Just about five miles from Kilbarrymeaden, a chief used to have regular skirmishes with a neighbouring clan from the Comeragh mountains, because they were continually stealing his animals. In one of these battles, his right hand man and best friend was seriously wounded and was in danger of death. The chief was sad and worried at the thought of losing his dear friend. The youth was tall, strong and fair and endeared himself to everyone. He always fought with great courage, always taking the front line of the battle.

He had many trophies hanging in his hut and he was also a talented poet. When he sang songs or played music on his harp outside his beehive dwelling on summer evenings, he always commanded silence. He was well loved by all, especially the young people of the district. When news of his injuries came to them, they all cried for him, as they knew it would only be days until he would be taken from them. The local healers tried to cure his injuries, but they were too serious for their knowledge and talent and the future looked bleak. The Chief stayed in his quarters, mourning for his dying friend and would not speak to anyone.

Then a wise old man who came from a mountain called Coumshinaun told him that only a short distance away lived a beautiful young princess. She was known to cure the ailments of many people. It was said that she could even bring them back to life if her God wished it so.

"That is unbelievable indeed," said the Chief and called his men around him, picking three of his most trusted to go to Kill and beg this Princess Ita to come to them in their hour of need. The three men set out and arrived in Kill in the early morning, but Ita was with the fishermen in Boatstrand and did not get back until evening. Still the men from Rossmede waited for her. They told her of the dire need they had of her powers and they pleaded with her to come as soon as she could, as the young man could not hold out much longer. After they had had food and rest, she sent them back home saying she would follow as soon as possible.

She arrived in the Rossmede fort late in the evening with twelve men as guards and the whole camp came out to meet her. The men were stony faced, the women looked anxious and the little children cried. Princess Ita dismounted from her horse and when the chief saw her, he knew in his heart that anything that was said about her must be true. His hopes began to rise. He gave her a warm welcome and she was taken to the bedside of the young man.

She prayed with him for some time and, to the amazement of everyone in the camp, he made a spectacular recovery. Then they prayed again, this time in thanksgiving for his deliverance and this was his first introduction to the True and Living God. Ita explained that it was not she but Jesus, the Son of the Living God who had healed him. He seemed to be overawed by her words and hungry for more knowledge of this God who was new to him and who had been so kind to him by delivering him from death. Ita stayed with him for several hours and he fell into a peaceful sleep. She then withdrew and sought rest herself.

The camp was awake at dawn, hoping for some good news and when the Chief made the startling announcement about the young manís deliverance, there was great excitement within the fort. The chiefís delight was great and he told Ita that anything she desired was hers.

"My own desire is to build a church where we can adore your true God," he said, "and that you would make Godís word known to my people."

The Chief summoned his builders and a church was soon built and ready for worship. Now Ita needed someone to look after it and so consulted the chief. He said that the young man, Cano, the one whom God had cured, should be given the responsibility, as he had spectacular knowledge and evidence of her God. She blessed the young man and gave him full authority, for she knew God would soon call her to another part of the country.

Ballylaneen

Princess Ita, daughter of Kennfoelad and Necta, Holy Woman and Christian inspiration, was about to move to Clashmore when some men from Ballylaneen, came to her, pleading with her to go to Ballylaneen with them. Their chief's son was dying, they told her, having been gored by a bull. Healers came to cure him but alas all they had done was to poison him. If she could not come, they pleaded with her, he would soon die. They wept openly as they told her that he was the only son and heir of their Chief. Ita asked about their leader and they assured her that he was a kind and gentle man. Then, the young Princess, accompanied by her bodyguard, consented to go with them.

After spending several hours praying with the sick boy, he sat up in bed, restored to health again. The people were overjoyed, but Ita again diverted their thanks and praise to Jesus, her God whom she lauded openly and often. It was too late in the day to continue her journey, so she stayed the night among the happy people. Afterwards, it was said that the boy whom she had cured had a divine light shining in him and, when he came of age, he travelled to Killeedy to Ita to become a student of hers. It was often wondered why Ita went off her direct route on her journey to Clashmore, but, even from the start of her life, she always answered Godís call.

St. Declan and St. Ita

According to menologic genealogy, Prince Declan and Princess Ita had the same pedigree, a common blood line descended from King Feidhlim the Lawgiver. Feidhlimís son who succeeded him was the celebrated Conn of the Hundred Battles, who began his reign in 122 or 123 AD. This monarch is said to have eventually fallen in battle on the plains of Cobha, killed by the Ulstermen. This was probably a district near the Hill of Tara. He was slain in 157 AD, having occupied the throne of Ireland for about 35 years.

Panel in the West Gable of Ardmore Cathedral showing Biblical scenes.

His son Fiachra never gained his inheritance to sit on the throne. However, he left three sons called Rossius, Angussius and Eugenius. Their general genealogy has been preserved in the life of Saint Declan. It provides the details which forms the story of their common ancestry and of the migration of the Decies.

At about the age of twenty, Ita travelled from Balylaneen and Kilmacthomas to Clashmore, where she built a church and also to Lismore and Ardmore. It is not known whether St. Declan sent for her, but he must have been in the need of assistance as he was nearing seventy years of age.

Ardmore was known at the time as the land of saints. While Ita had much to tell him about her ships and shipbuilding and her schools and churches, Declan too had much to tell Ita about God and the people among whom he worked. He too would have known of the power of the Druids and how to deal with them. He must have known where those desperate people lived who feared the Druids and encouraged her to go that way and help them. It is also known he gave her the rites of the church to make her a Holy Woman. She became his trusted companion and helper and travelled far and wide in the Blackwater Valley.

The site of St. Ita's Church, Clashmore

One day as Ita sat on a flat stone on St. Patrick's ancient road, she saw some Holy men, who had a child with them. Seeing him, Ita wept bitterly. The Holy men demanded why she cried at seeing them. 'Blessed is the hour' she answered "in which that youth in your company was born, for no one shall go to Hell from the

Kilmeady, Clashmore

cemetery in which he will be buried. But alas for me, I cannot be buried therein."

The men asked to which cemetery she referred and she replied that it was in Mochuda's cemetery, 'though it is not yet consecrated', for she knew that a Holy Man would in a later century found a monastery and church there.

"He will be honoured and famous in time to come," said Ita and, in the fullness of time, this all came to pass for the youth. Afterward, he became a monk under Muchuda and is buried in the Monastic cemetery of Lismore. As Ita had foretold, like Clonmacnoise, Iona and Glendalough, Lismore became one of Ireland's most desired resting places of Kings and Bishops. Murdcheartach, Monarch of Ireland and St Belus, Primate in Armagh found a grave in this Holy soil.

A Boy Called Flann

In Ita's time, a boy named Flann lived in Lismore. He was young and strong. He had a wolf-like claw on his left hand and always hid it from sight of the people. He was ridiculed by others and the boys tormented him and even threw stones at him. His deformity was blamed for everything bad that happened in the village and he had a miserable childhood. On one occasion, some cattle were killed by lightning and the poor youth was even blamed for that. Many a night he cried himself to sleep and often wondered what would happen to him if he did something really bad.

The boy's condition was a great grief to his loving parents and his mother's heart was very sore. She did not know what to do if he left his home to live in the nearby wood, as he sometimes said he would to flee from the torment.

A group of young men from the village formed a gang to hunt him down and he had to move into a cave in the Knockmealdown mountains to be away from his tormentors. He could only visit his loving parents by night, as he felt his life would be in danger if he came in daylight. His poor mother always had food and clothes ready for him and her heart bled for him, for she was both lonely herself and worried for him.

He spent many months in that lonely cave and sometimes his father would visit him and bring him clothes and food. He wondered if his exile would ever end and would ask himself why he was born with this animal's claw. Now, the animals were his best friends and he could almost talk to them. Was he really meant to be an animal, living in the wild for the rest of his life?

They came to the cave at night and kept him warm and he attended to their injuries. He put splints on their broken legs and when young cubs got caught among the rocks, he freed them and he knew their mothers were grateful.

On one occasion, he came across a wolf lying dying, cold and hungry. Flann took him to the cave, fed and nursed him back to full health. He looked on him as he would a dog, a companion and man's best friend. Wherever he went, the wolf went with him and showed him sights no man had ever seen. Sometimes as the animals gathered round, he spoke to them and told them stories. They seemed to understand him. This erased some of his pain, restored his self respect and his fidelity always remained, as his mother had taught him. He never harboured ill-will towards anyone. He may not always have enjoyed it, but he endured life as best he could. Sometimes he felt lonely and wondered if his exile would ever end.

Then his sad and lonely poor mother heard of a wonderful woman called Princess Ita in Clashmore. She put on her shawl and set out to find her and pay her a visit. She told the Holy Woman her sad story and asked for her help. She could not describe where her son was, but Ita assured her that God would guide her to the worthy cause.

Next evening, Ita mounted her horse and rode straight to the cave. She found the young man sitting inside, with a little kid across his knee.

"Hello Flann," she greeted him, "God be with you."

He was surprised to see this lovely princess and could only stare at her as he had not seen a woman for a long time. She chatted about the animals and the stories he told her about them made them almost human. The stories Ita told Flann about God in return, filled him with delight. She paid him several visits, and on one occasion, looked at his claw, took off the hair, cut the nails and assured him that in God's time, it would be normal. She also told him she would not condone anybody tormenting him again.

He went back to the Rath with the Princess and, with her guidance, he became a master craftsman and built many beehive houses for Ita and for her people. He was admired by all in his new fulfilling life.

St. Patrick's Ancient Road

As Ita walked along St. Patrick's Road, she saw two tired and weary men sawing timber and stopped to speak with them. They told her that as young boys, their father had hired them out to a knave of a chief for money, which he needed badly to buy food for the rest of his children. The young boys had to work from daylight 'til dark, with just bread and water for nourishment and now, they hadn't eaten for several days. Ita was very angry when she heard their sad story and told them to go to their master and ask him to release them. They went, but he refused and just scoffed at them.

A month later as Ita was passing by again, she saw the two young men working as before. Sadly, they told her, their master would not release them.

" I will deal with him myself," she said.

The chief was away enjoying a huge feast with his friends and when he returned, all his cattle were sick. He made enquiries and heard of Ita's visit and her sympathy for the two boys. He came to Ita begging her forgiveness and, as a result of their meeting, he too became a Christian and gave her great help.

On another occasion, she came upon two whose hands were red and raw from sawing timber. It was a very hard work as the saw had little edge on it. Ita blessed the saw for them and they continued their work without difficulty. They thanked Ita and became obedient servants to the Christian way.

A Chieftain's Call

A chieftain called Mighty Chub sent for Declan to cure his only daughter who had been poisoned, a common occurence at that time and she was in danger of death. Meanwhile his wife sent to Clashmore for Ita. Both came and they met on the road to Youghal and travelled to the sick girl together. Declan went to the chieftain to advise him and his wife brought St. Ita to the sick girl's quarters.

After some time with the girl, Ita restored her to health. The chieftain asked Declan when he was going to see his daughter and when he heard that Ita and not Declan had cured his daughter, he was not very pleased. He did not want to see Ita or talk to her or even for her to talk to his wife. Declan tried to explain that it was God who had cured her and neither Ita nor himself. Declan mounted his horse and rode towards Ardmore, while Ita returned to Clashmore.

She had several bodyguards with her as her life was still in danger from the 'Mad Prince', as he was now called. Still, she never worried and often took wild chances. Sometimes she liked to ride fast, as she was a good horse woman, but men found it difficult to understand how she could be so reckless. However, she trusted God to take care of her.

Ita learned a great deal from her elder, Declan, on his saintly life. He told her about the Druids and how she should deal with them and she was always keen to learn. She made many new missions for him along the Blackwater as far as Youghal.

In Clonpriest, Declan and his people built a church and he had it named Ita's church. There, she had the reputation of curing illnesses and ailments. Even among the Pagans whom she helped without question, people knew she was specially sanctified by the Holy Spirit of God. She spent even more of her time with them, played with their children and showed them new games to play.

Rock of Cashel, an early fortication and Monastic site
which was visited by St. Declan.

Anoh Caomh - King of Cashel

King Anoh Caomh of Cashel was in his fifties when he was crowned King. There was more than one claimant to the throne and one of the objections to him was that he was not married and had no heir to the kingdom of Cashel. He was a great warrior, however and no one dared to challenge him to a sword fight. At the end of a day's hunting, he would always have the biggest deer, with the longest antlers. No other man could boast of so many kills of wild boar or any other animals than he. The succession was still in hot dispute and Declan was sent for as a guarantor to the agreement that if Anoh Caomh had no heir, the crown would fall to his cousin.

Years passed and he proved to be a good and just king. He never fell in love and did not take a wife. It was not for the want of a woman, beautiful or not, for several wealthy men from all over Ireland came to him, offering him their lovely daughters, with land, money and jewels. Many times, as he was out hunting at night, sitting around the campfire, he would listen to the storytellers. One night he heard them telling about a young princess who was with the holy man Declan. Her beauty knew no bounds, they said and her bravery was great. She was guarded by eight men as she rode through the countryside, often outriding those looking after her, which worried them very much. When they would ask her why she would behave in such a reckless manner, she would only smile.

The princess was always guarded and it was said that she refused the hand of a prince of Tara, who became very angry with her. He swore he would crush her father in battle and take her prisoner. Her father and his warriors beat him off several times, but he swore he would prevail in the end.

The King of Cashel listened to this for several nights. The more he thought about it, the more it stayed in his mind. He sent a courier to Ardmore, inviting the holy man Declan and the celebrated young Holy Woman who was with him, to visit him in Cashel. They went to meet him the following month and King Caomh put on a great feast in their honour. Declan and Ita were given the place of honour and beside the king's table there were many great singers, storytellers, magicians and acrobats from near and far. Only a king could put on such a feast.

Later in the night it was suggested that the princess must sing. It was to be requested by the king and Ita was never one to hold back when at a celebration or a feast, as she liked everyone to enjoy themselves. She requested a harp and it was quickly brought to her.

People did not know what to expect from Ita and, as she prepared to sing, silence fell on the hall. Her voice started low and her words could barely be heard. Her song sounded as if it were coming from the past, from another age. Some could understand, more could not. The silence was now complete, broken only by the low tones of Ita and the sweet music of her harp. With each song she modulated her voice to suit the tune.

In her second song, the words became mellow and soulful and when she finished, there was an overawed silence and even the king himself did not stir for some moments.

Then he touched Declan's hand, asking if it would be fitting if he asked for the princess's hand in marriage. Declan looked at the king beneath his eyelashes and he suddenly realised that their king was in love for the first time in his life. He also knew the chances of his winning the hand of Princess Ita were slim indeed. Don't let your hopes rise too high, said the holy man as he moved away to allow Ita sit next to the king, who complimented her on her lovely singing. It was enchanting. It would lift any person's heart just to hear that lovely voice.

Slowly Ita raised her eyes to the level of the King's face. He looked different to her now and spoke a little unsurely.

"Could it . . . , would it be . . ., I am asking you to be my wife and the Queen of my realm" he said finally. The princess gave her answer without hesitating.

"I can not accept your proposal Highness, but you do me a great honour. It makes my heart sad if it causes you any pain. I have offered myself to Christ, Son of the Living God. I am known as the bride of Christ. I have heard many great stories in praise of you and I know you are a good king to your people. They love you very much and you are held in high regard. We both have our paths willed by God: you to go one way, I the other, each doing the will of God"

"I accept what you say as the will of God," said the King, sadly. "All I now ask for is your friendship. If ever I need you, you must come."

The feast went on for a long time, but that brought an end to the talk of marriage and, in time, Ita returned to Ardmore with Declan.

On a later occasion, when she was returning from visiting her nephew Mochoemog, Ita visited again. When she told him her nephew was having trouble, he became very angry.

"Holy Woman, please accept from me a gift here in my kingdom. You can have as much land as you need for setting up a monastery community now or at any future date."

Ita again visited King Anoh Caomh when he was dying and laid her holy hands on him. He passed to his reward smiling and happy.

Tobar Ocht

Ita's Well is in West Waterford at Guile on the coast near Piltown, Youghal, just a few miles from the site of St. Ita's Church, Kilmeady, Clashmore. The well has been looked after by William Roche and his family for generations and has been known for its cures, especially for the ailments of children and the elderly. Children with illness were sent to the well for nine days in succession to pray. The recommended prayers are the Hail Mary and Gloria to be recited five times and then a drink to be taken of the pure and clear water of the well.

When a child was restored to health, mothers would then go for nine days and say many rosaries at the well in thanksgiving. One elderly man with a severely infected throat, was so eager and had such strong faith, that he would run the last hundred yards to the well, take a tin mug, fill it with water three times and drink it. He would declare himself improved immediately, thanks to the Virgin.

The Cliffs at Guile, Piltown, Co. Waterford beside Tober Ocht.

Tobar Ocht - St. Ita's Well at Guile, Piltown, Co. Waterford.

Declan and Ita would meet here and a large crowd would gather to hear and see those two great preachers at this lovely spot near the sea. Declan would arrive by boat with two holy men, while Ita would come on horseback, accompanied by men to guard her, as her life was always in danger from the Wicked Prince.

The elderly Declan would speak for a short time and then introduce the young maiden from the Suir side. Ita would speak to them enthusiastically and sometimes amusingly. She would speak about the Blessed Trinity, about the love God had for humankind and how he had given His beloved Son to die on the cross of Calvary. She would speak of how Christ's Mother Mary suffered while looking at her beloved Son die in agony.

"What can we do to relieve that suffering," she would ask. "Through the great love God has for you, His people, our Father in Heaven would like you to give food and clothes to those less well off than yourselves. Any person who has taken wrongfully from the people, they must return it in its entirety to its rightful owners. God would frown on those people who would scowl on the face of mankind, or look on them with enmity. Do to others as you would like others to do to you," she would quote from the Gospel.

Later, when Ita too had spoken, Declan would sit back pleased with his young kinswoman and, together, they would lay hands on the people to bring give blessings upon them.

Abbot Bishop Colman of Lismore

Because of his severely fading sight, for several years Bishop Colman of Lismore had to refrain from administering to his flock. Ita was prevailed upon to help him and she restored his sight so that he could return to guide and minister to his people. As Bishop, he ordained many youths to become Holy Men and through his ministry, he became known throughout Ireland.

Colman, Abbot and Bishop, was born on the banks of the river Blackwater and became a monk in Ardmore. After completing his studies, he was consecrated Bishop of Lismore, though he was somewhat unwilling to take on the onerous task. Because of the importance of Lismore as a seat of learning at the time, one of the finest in Europe, he had many monks under his jurisdiction.

One morning he woke up to find he had lost his sight, but conscious of his responsibilities, he carried on as best as he could with the help of his brother monks. He often communicated with Declan, but they never discussed the Bishop's sight, concentrating instead on religious matters.

When Ita came to Ardmore on a visit to Declan, she befriended Abbot Colman and had many discussions with him. One day she asked him if she could pray to Jesus to restore his sight. She pointed out to him that he could do God's work better if he had his sight.

"God took away my sight for a good reason," Colman told Ita philosophically, "and God will restore it if it be His will. Do what you think is best, my girl."

Ita started a vigil at eight o'clock in the evening, praying to Jesus until eight the next morning. The Abbot woke early and told his monks to open the windows leaving in God's fresh air. Immediately two white doves flew in and landed on Colman, one on each shoulder. Colman took one dove in his hand exclaiming what lovely birds they had been sent. He then continued what he had been saying as if nothing had happened, accepting that his sight had been miraculously restored.

He continued to rule as Abbot for many years and asked Ita if she would give homilies for his monks. On different occasions she spoke on the love which Jesus had for them, as well as the value of thought and also on the courage to do the will of God.

Clonpriest

The site of St. Ita's Church in Clonpriest

One evening as Ita visited Declan's people in Clonpriest, when the weather was rough and windy, a cry went up from the shore. Three young men were out at sea and in grave danger due to the storm. They were in the water, and unable to swim. Ita ordered a boat to be brought out, but the men protested saying 'do not put your life in danger, no one can survive in those conditions'.

As the thunder and lightning storm prevailed, Ita persisted. She and two of the bravest of the men took to the boat and it rocked and swayed as they pulled towards the struggling young men in the water. One of her helpers fell overboard, but she and the other man managed to get him back on board again. Finally, they reached the sinking boat, but none of the youths were on with it.

Suddenly, the sea calmed and, on Ita's instructions, her companions dived into the water, which they had not done before. One by one, the three shipwrecked youths were taken from the water by the two men and they showed little sign of life. Ita nursed them, praying as she worked and slowly life returned to the three limp bodies.

By the time they returned, a large crowd had gathered on the shore and they all acclaimed her and her feat. One of those saved was the son of the Chief of the nearby fort at Clonpriest, his cousin from Pilmore fort and a third from Aglish, over the border in Co. Waterford who had all gone out in the boat.

The fathers of the three youths were chieftains and also brothers and they resolved to make known the great actions of Ita among the people of Aglish, Clashmore, Lismore and Ardmore and the lands between. This made her ministry to the people's needs all the easier. The chieftain in Aglish called all his people and instructed them to build a church in her honour. Six months later, when she again visited Aglish, she was greatly surprised by what she found and thanked God for the loyalty and gratitude of the people. To this day, that lovely site is venerated by its people.

Declan was pleased with his kinswoman and her acts of kindness. He was proud of the way she used her spiritual powers on behalf the people and the way she ministered to their needs, both spiritual and physical. She had many difficulties travelling the ancient roads of Sixth Century Munster, as she helped to bring the Christian message to the people and be herself, a fitting symbol of spiritual life to those whom she wished to convert.

There were many signs of her works left behind as she moved to the next place. In Lismore a crippled man left his crutch and walked

AGLISH

away. In Clashmore, a woman had her finger straightened and, elsewhere, a man got relief from bad pains. All of these cures had a positive effect on the people and gave them cause for peaceful reflection.

Back in Clonpriest, the people lived for the days when Ita would visit them and she showed them how to tame wild donkeys and how they could use them to ride on and for work. She told them to be kind to all the birds; to feed them when winter came and be especially kind to lame dogs who were man's best friends. All animals, she told them, were God's creatures.

All were very happy until the princess got bad news. Someone had declared war on her father and now she would soon have to leave this peaceful countryside and bid farewell to Declan too.

Battle of Coolfin

Loe Ghuire, Prince of Tara, returned to the Suirside to once more see if he could capture Princess Ita and take her away from her father King Kennfoelad. This is what Ita's father was afraid might happen, but he had his brother Prince Kennfoelad to help him fight the foe. They were able to muster up three hundred and fifty men between them, but Loe Ghuire on his side, thought that two hundred men would be sufficient to defeat the King and take possession of his lovely daughter, Princess Ita.

With the joint forces of his brother, the King had the upper hand. Loe Ghuire had to give ground and quickly retreat. He returned back across the Suir via Kilmeaden and further back to the hill of Fionn McCumhal in Leinster where he recuperated for some time. As he lay outside in his hammock, he became furious and looked on King Kennfoelad as only a temporary obstacle and a lucky fighter who was getting on in years. Here he, Loe Ghuire was a mighty prince, a great warrior who had already won many battles and he would take what he thought was rightfully his.

He could visualize the beautiful woman who by now would have become tall and mature and he devised another plan to beat the foolish King. If Ita still refused to marry him he would abduct her, take her with him, come what may and he dared anyone to try to stop him. Loe Ghuire wondered who this Heavenly Prince Jesus could be, that he should be held in such high regard. He would deal with him in his own time, he decided, when he had formulated a suitable plan.

Battle at Lackamore Cross, Clashmore

Loe Ghuire could think of nothing but how he would gain revenge on Princess Itaís father for failing to deliver her to him. As time went on he thought of ways to soothe his hurt pride and they were mainly at the expense of Ita and her father. He would let them see he was the mighty Loe Ghuire, Prince of Tara.

In time, Loe Ghuire once more attacked Princess Ita's Fort, this time at dawn. King Kennfoelad along with his brother Prince Kennfoelad and their kinsman Conla found that they were outnumbered almost two to one. They were good Celtic fighters, however and were hopeful that they could turn the tide at the end of the day.

Loe Ghuire, on the other hand, was sure that victory would be his. He had his brother's forces, with many great fighters from Leinster and paid warriors as well. They were promised great rewards if they were successful and could capture the lovely princess. Loe Ghuire wanted her unharmed, but he was hungry for revenge and he would make everyone pay the price of his humiliation. He would hunt them to the ends of the earth if necessary.

He would also have the lovely princess, he vowed, but this was also a contest between Leinster and Munster. Ita had been a mere girl when he last saw her in Kilmeaden, but now, she must be a mature woman after those five years. He would not even make her his wife now and it would serve her right. He wondered why she never married this Prince Jesus of whom she spoke so much, and to whom she said she was promised. Even if she had, he would deal with him too. He would take her back to Tara and would have a good time at her expense. He who laughs last laughs the longest, he often thought to himself.

Loe Ghuire had his plan well laid out. He would draw King Kennfoelad's men away from the fort, knowing that they would put all their warriors on the battlefield. He would then send ten men back to the fort on horseback and take the princess by force. He would fight a skirmish and then retreat, inducing the defenders to follow. He did this a few times, drawing the defenders ever further away from their fort until there was sufficient space between Ita's home and the battlefield for his plan to be put into action. Then the real fighting began.

Meanwhile, Prince Loe Ghuire's men went to the fort to capture Ita, only to find she was not there. She had chosen to be near her fighting men. The prince was thwarted once again and his dismay and rage as he received the news at Lackamore Cross was fierce to behold. He swore he would soon be avenged and that Kennfoelad and his men would all get their just rewards. Not one of these Decies men would live to tell about this battle. After all, he had the advantage as his men outnumbered King Kennfoelad's, two to one. He urged his warriors on to bring the fight to a finish.

But the Suir men fought like true Celtic warriors. They were conscious that if they were defeated, they would not only lose their lives but their tribe would cease to exist as a fighting force. They also knew what the fate of their beautiful princess would be in the hands of the mad, crazy prince. All his acts were shameful and wrong.

But Loe Ghuire was angrier than ever now and blamed his men for their inability to bring the battle to a speedy close. Still, he would not have long to wait and fierce battle was renewed with no quarter given. Blow for blow and man for man, nothing was left to chance, The King and his brother fought as never before, but fought as kings do. The battle went on for days, never stopping until nightfall, to start again at dawn. The battle swayed back and forth, with both sides holding the advantage by turn.

Then Ita came on to the battlefield, worried about her kinspeople. She watched in fear as her father fought with a strong skilled foe. He seemed to be getting the upper hand of his opponent and was about to strike the final blow, when another warrior came behind him and stabbed him on the left side of his back. He fell mortally wounded from the foul deed.

His daughter, the Princess, was petrified and stood in a trance for a few moments. Then, as if guided by the hand of God and without any prior knowledge of swords, like a streak of lightning, she grasped her father's weapon. She moved through the battlefield striking right and left and, as each blow struck, an enemy warrior fell, miraculously, there was no blood. One by one they fell around her, until they amounted to thirteen or fourteen men. Prince Loe Ghuire watched Ita and her fighting skill made her even more desirable to him. He was more determined than ever to have her, but he feared she might be killed if they continued to fight. It would deprive him of his prize. Now that her father had fallen, it would make it easier to fight his people again.

King Kennfoelad's blood ebbed away as he lay dying at what is now known as Lackamore Cross. He knew the enemy had

The site of the battle of Lackamore where King Kennfoelad was killed.

withdrawn and this would give his people more time to make plans. As he lay in the arms of his loving daughter, Ita for whom he had willingly sacrificed his life, he was barely able to speak, but asked his warriors which of them would be her guardian. They answered one and all that each would be her guardian until the last one fell. The Princess wanted to continue the fight with her people, but Prince Kennfoelad, the King's brother, promised that he would take Ita out of danger.

The Prince gave a short oration, recalling their exploits by the River Suir.

"As far as we are concerned," he told the assembled warriors, "we will fight until we defeat the enemy. We will consider ourselves God's army and ask him to guide us in battle."

Princess Ita was sad as she rode away from Lackamore Cross with her guards into the night. The King and his fallen warriors were buried at Lackamore Cross by the local Chieftain and the people of Clashmore. Twenty-three of the Kilmeadan men and thirty-three of the Leinster men lost their lives at this battle.

Ita Leaves the Fort at Gortroe

After the battle with Loe Ghuire, Ita traveled to a place now called Gortroe, and arrived at a safe house in a friendly fort. There she was made welcome and a rest room was prepared for her. She was given food by the Chieftain's wife, who became very emotional as she told Ita her sad story. She had twin boys, both of whom were very healthy, until one day while playing on the riverbank, one of them fell into the water. He was rescued in time, but was now very ill. The mother's sorrow seemed endless.

Princess Ita finished her meal and then asked if she could see the sick boy. For several days and nights previously, she had had no rest having had only three hours sleep after the saddest day of her life. She had seen her father killed and then continued to fight his battle and now she had to think of someone else. She asked to be taken to the boy who was ill. She took him in her arms and said prayers for his recovery. When she became weary and fell asleep with the child in her arms, she was left to rest for a few hours. When her guards reluctantly came to wake her, they found that the little twin had recovered and was again as healthy as his brother.

The Chieftain and his lovely young wife were full of gratitude towards Ita. They idolised her and were sad that she had to leave so quickly. The Chieftain asked what they could do for Ita, declaring that nothing would be too great or too small for him to do in return for the health of his child. Ita told him she would like him to build a church in the place now known as Gortroe, a few miles west of Youghal, Co. Cork, in honour of her Christian people and he immediately agreed.

For whatever reason, the Church was not built at the time and it was not until the late Nineteenth Century, when St. Ita appeared to Mrs. Hannah O'Neill of that locality, was the project resurrected. Through her promotion of the idea and the dedicated work of Munster people, at home and abroad, the dream of a Church was finally brought to fruition in the early years of the Twentieth Century.

The church was built in Gortroe, where the battle took place between Loe Ghuire and Prince Kennfoelad, and where the present church stands.

Gortroe, Youghal

Prince Kennfoelad and his men moved along marshy ground, making slow headway. They were aware that if they were to defeat the angry prince, every decision would have to be a good one. Their fighting men were outnumbered, two to one and they had sent ten men to guard the princess, hoping she would be far away by now. They knew they must out-think and outwit Loe Ghuire to have any chance of defeating him. They knew that the Princess was well known in this part of the country and that people would look favourably on them. They therefore decided to ambush Loe Ghuire when he would least expect it.

They knew they had about six hours to prepare, so they found a piece of hollowed ground with bushes all around. They refreshed themselves in the river, ate whatever food they had brought and took a short rest. They sent out their scouts to find where the enemy was.

Meanwhile, Prince Loe Ghuire was pressing his men on as he was in a hurry to catch up. He would punish all those who had opposed him and would spare no one. He would show them what a great warrior he was and would claim his prize of the elusive princess. Despite his men being physically and mentally fatigued, he drove them on. Some resented the harsh treatment and knew that this was not the way Kennfoelad treated his men.

As Loe Ghuire travelled on, he came near to where prince Kennfoelad and his leading man, that great Decies nobleman, Conla waited near Clonpriest. When Loe Ghuire's force came near, the Kilmeaden men rose and surprised them. After some of them were killed, the Leinster men were about to turn tail and run, but their leader rallied them.

Still Ita's men were heavily outnumbered and, after four hours of fierce fighting, the strain was beginning to tell on Prince Kennfoelad's men. He ordered them to pull back towards the place now called Gortroe - meaning red or bloody field - so named after the battle that was fought there.

At this stage, many of the fighting men had fallen on the field of battle, but Prince Kennfoelad knew his niece should be safely away by now. This confidence added to his skills as a Celtic warrior, but, as he had offered his men to God as the first Christian warriors, he could not consider defeat, even at this late hour.

On the other side, the Mad Prince, seeing the Waterford men pull

back towards Gortroe, knew the battle was within his grasp. Victory, as well as the lovely princess would be his, he thought. Every man that fell by his sword was one step nearer and he jubilantly urged his men

The site of the battle of Gortroe

on with promises of rich rewards for that one last effort which
would win the day.

Castle built where St. Ita stayed overnight near Gortroe

Still the Decies men held their ground. Stubbornness was
neutralising the fight, but what the Prince did not know was that
two other forces were coming from two different directions. As the
fight swayed to and fro, men from Clonpriest and men from
Pilmore entered the battle and then the slaughter began in earnest.
It was not long before their fresh presence was felt, but yet, it was
still doubtful which way it would end.

Soon after, it looked as if the Leinster men were beginning to
draw back towards the sea. The Mad Prince noticed this and knew
that unless he could initiate a decisive and drastic course of action,
the end would be dreadful for him. He could see his prize, the
lovely Princess slipping away from him. The Cork men were very
dynamic and were very effective in mowing down the enemy. Yet,
the Prince's very determination would not allow him give in too
easily. His endurance was srong and he tried to motivate his men to
fight on.

Prince Kennfoelad and his forces were beginning to engulf them now. The Kilmeaden, Clonpriest and Pilmore men would talk of this fight for many years to come and it would create a special bond between them. Now, the fight was getting easier as their enthusiasm again strengthened and finally, after seven hours of bloody battle, it was all over rather quickly.

It was evening and foggy when they went to look for the defeated Prince among the fallen, but he was missing. He could not be found either dead or alive in the mist of the evening, for the cunning and wily Prince had escaped with a few of his men in a boat, leaving the rest of his warriors wounded and dying on the bloody battlefield.

The men of the victorious clans were glad to sit and rest where the fighting had finished. Some of them sang songs of victory and more just chatted and relived the details of the fight. Suddenly, a group of the brave Kilmeaden Christian fighting men circled a fallen warrior on the field, talking in whispers. Their brave leader, Prince Kennfoelad lay mortally wounded. He had been struck in the final moments of the battle and now looked up to see the faces of the warriors who had fought by his side. A hush came over the field and grown men cried as the news spread. Though a victim of the battle, the dying prince was thankful that his niece, the Princess Ita had escaped to continue her work for the living and true God.

The slain warriors were buried where they fell and the great leader and fighter, Prince Kennfoelad was buried close to where Ita would ask for a church to be built years later.

Crossbarry, Chieftain Naoise

Chief Naoise, the leader of the Killeady tribe was thirty-three years old and married with two daughters. Now, his wife of twenty was pregnant again and the chieftain was hoping for a son. He had more regard and concern for the expected baby than he had for its mother. In due course, his wife went into labour, but the midwife was not able to deliver the baby. The chief was frantic, for after waiting so long for a son, it seemed he was now going to lose it. Who could he call; where could he go for help? It seemed hopeless.

Then two wise old men came and told him about a godly woman named Ita who was able to work wonders. She spoke about a living God who wanted to help people if they listened and some said she even worked miracles. Ita was in the city of Cork, they said, and should be sent for.

The Chief ordered ten men to mount and go and look for her in Cork. They found her as they had been told and were very surprised that the princess looked so beautiful. They were even more surprised when she consented to go with them. They told her the child would be lucky to be alive when they got back, so Ita advised them not to delay. She arrived a day later and helped the midwife to deliver the baby boy but, alas, it was already dead. The chieftain had to be taken out of the room in grief and all the women were wailing.

Ita bade them be quiet and picked up the baby in her arms, rocking him to and fro for several hours. "Holy, holy Jesus, son of the Virgin, give life to this child," she prayed. "Sweet Jesus give him light; Jesus, this baby has committed no sin, come to him and heal him."

All was quiet and then Ita smiled and handed the baby to his mother who lay on a couch. "Your child has life in him now," Ita said and, as the baby gave a loud cry she continued: "That is life."

The chieftain was overjoyed and offered the princess anything she would ask for.

Crossbarry where the child of the local Druid was saved

"I want nothing for myself," said Ita, "what I want from you is a church and a school in which to teach your children."

The Chief was as good as his word and in a couple of months, Ita

Crossbarry Church site

had her church and in another month, she had the school. Very soon the children flocked to her and she taught men and women to become teachers themselves. They were also taught the word of God, which, to Ita, was the most important part of her work.

When word of this latest wondrous happening reached the Druids, they were furious. They saw the Holy Woman take souls from their control and slaves from their bondage and they resolved to do something about her. Who was she? Did she think she had greater power than the spirits to whom they directed their prayers? They ranted and raved and sent her messages to frighten her. Itaís own men were ready to defend her, come what may and the subject was discussed in the fort. The chieftain, amid controversy, demanded silence.

"It was I who sent for the virgin to be brought here," he said. "It is I who put her in danger. It was my son she brought back to life. It is my men who are going to defend her."

Forty of the chieftain's best men were selected to defend her. The Druids sent word, written in a fierce hand, that at dusk, when they had won the battle, they would set the fort on fire and burn all within. The Druids were ranged in order, their hands uplifted, invoking their gods, pouring forth horrible incantations. The chieftain's men stood for a while stupefied in amazement, as if their limbs would not move. They were bemused as they looked at one another and felt embarrassed and annoyed by their lack of energy. They recovered themselves and with deeds of valour in mind, they rushed the enemy with swords drawn. As they came near, without striking their opponents, fire poured from the Druids hands. The men were lifted off their feet and thrown in all directions, against walls and trees. Their leader was thrown against a tree with a spike protruding from it, which went through his back. He lay dying with fourteen of his men injured.

This put fear into everybody and the Druids now had the upper hand. A tall ghostly figure with long fingernails and long shoes with turned up toes stepped out from the group.

"As the leader of the Druids, hear me, hear me. You have seen the great power of our gods. We took slaves before and now we want more sacrifices. Our gods are great and you have to obey their commands. We are invincible. Where is this fabled virgin of yours? Let her come out with her famous Gods," they jeered her. "Those Gods are false. Why can't she come out?"

Then the beautiful Ita stepped out from the fort. Three shining lights glowed all around her. She stood in silence for a few moments, then loud and clear, her voice rang out over the crowd.

Crossbarry Well

"Depart you evil spirits, begone. Do not deceive yourselves for Jesus is the King of all of the universe. The Holy Trinity of Father, Son and Holy Spirit are now among these people. They will always

Site of School where St. Ita and her Holy Women taught for 140 years. It was later a coach-house and is now a licenced premises.

be protected from evil spirits. Go, before the fire you used on my people, consumes you."

The Druids gathered in a circle. Their babble could be heard. They broke up, then departed, looking very dejected.

The Druids of Finnbarry

The high priest of the Druids had a disagreement with his wife and she left him, bringing their six year old daughter with her and went to stay with her sister, who lived near the river. As the child played on the banks of the river with other little friends, she slipped and fell in. Just then, her father happened to arrive, only to see his daughter being carried away in the current. He ran after her along the bank, accompanied by a crowd of people and just as he was about to overtake her, she disappeared.

He threw off his cloak and jumped into the water fully clothed. He was a powerful swimmer but he was too late as she had sunk under the water. Seeing her on the riverbed, he dived under and quickly brought her up and swam to the bank. Willing hands took her from him but alas, she was dead. Everything possible was done to restore her to life. As she lay on the ground beside the river, every god the Druids had known were called upon. Every known magic word was said to revive her, but it was not to be.

Her mother and father were broken hearted. They put their arms around one another and cried. The father gathered their daughter in his arms and carried the dead girl home. They promised never to disagree again. They sat in despair. If only . . . . . they thought.

The chieftain of Kileedy, now a Godly man, heard the news and went to console the grieving parents. He suggested they should send for the great Princess Ita. The Druid had nothing to lose and nothing could be too great or too small if she could save his daughter. He asked the chieftain to go and fetch her, but the Chief replied that it would be better if he went himself.

So the brokenhearted Druid took twenty of his men and went to Ita. He went down on his knees and beseeched her to come. She agreed and he promised he would forsake all his gods and that he and his people would worship the true and living God. In the space of one day, Ita travelled from Killeedy in Limerick to Cross Barry on her white horse, with five men to guard her. When she arrived, only Ita and the Druid went to where the dead girl lay.

They both spent many hours praying, the Druid repeating the prayers as if he had known them all his life. Then as their entreaties came to an end, Ita spoke by herself.

"Father, Son and Holy Spirit, Blessed Trinity, Holy Trinity, arise little Angel," she said to the girl, "your father is waiting for you." Suddenly, the girl sat up dazed and bewildered. Then she smiled and clung to Ita. Her father took her in his arms and cried and her mother was called. She was overjoyed and, in turn, hugged and kissed the child who had been given back to her.

The Druids and the Gaels had gathered together and had waited for hours for news. Now, the overjoyed parents took the girl by the hand and went outside. The crowd gasped in amazement when they saw the young child alive and were impressed by the power which Ita had brought and had used in restoring the child to her parents. This was one more proof that Ita spoke for, and was the instrument of the One, True God and that her God was vastly more powerful than those of the ancient Druids.

Finbar - Crossbarry

More than fourteen centuries have passed since Finbar was baptized Jeremiah Lorken, born somewhere near Cross Barry, Crooktown, near Killeedy in the year 520. His father was visiting his uncle in Goughane Barra.

On Tuesday 25th September in the year 523 Ita was told by Jesus to take care of Finbar and look after his welfare. He was then just three years old, but he immediately looked on her as his second mother. When she talked of God, he always understood what she meant. As a second mother, she also advised him on many other things besides.

As a youth, he liked to fish and sail his boat on the Owenabee river with the other young boys of his village. Ita knew that he was a devout child and he was always happy when she came to visit him. She could see how he was different from other boys and she knew Jesus had a special interest in him. When he was twelve, and just as Ita was coming to her last years of teaching, he asked to be

The little Church at
Gougane Barra

James Dunphy
and his
grandaughter
Emma Dunphy at
Gougane Barra

taken into Ita's school to study to become a holy man of God. He walked across the mountains to Killeedy in Limerick and joined with the other young men who had pledged themselves to God under Ita's direction.

Life was agreeable for those who aspired to the religious life and Finbar was happy there among similarly minded people, in pursuit of truth and learning about the One, True God of whom Ita spoke so much.

At that time, there were evil men in Cork who had the power to see that the youth Finbar, in time to come, would win many souls for God, taking them away from their harvest. Thinking he would be at home, they decided to burn him out, along with his family, not knowing he had already departed for Ita's school to become a holy man.

About the same time, after some years in Killeedy, Finbar decided to go home to Cross Barry to again make contact with his family. When he arrived, he found his home on fire and his beloved father and mother caught in the blaze. He was powerless to rescue them and they perished in the blaze. He was distraught and, as it was the dusk of the evening, he was petrified with nowhere to go for the night. However, two holy men took care of him and brought him back to Cork with them late that night.

He knew he had escaped with the protection of the Lord and gave thanks for his delivery and prayed regularly for the souls of his parents. After six months in Cork, he returned to Ita to continue his training. When he had completed his preparation for a life of devout service to God and his people, he returned to Cork to begin his ministry. Ita sent ten men with him to guard him as she did not wish for a repeat of the earlier attempt on his life. Tradition says that he was ordained by a Bishop named Forterues and that it was the work and encouragement of Finbar which drew people to the area and made Cork a city.

Killeedy Hill, Crossbarry

Finbar died in or about 603 and was buried in the grounds of his beloved Cathedral. There, his name and image are carved on the face of the Bishop's Throne.

Chief Molicmor at Millstreet

The Druids from Britain had a strong influence over the Gaelic tribes. They had great fortifications and their tribal headquarters at Kilcummin spread out over Cullen at the foot of The Paps mountains, around Millstreet and Muskerry and was renamed Kilmeady. The Gaelic tribes were gravely disturbed for they were continually persecuted by the Druids who destroyed their harvest, stole their animals, burned their crops and muddied their waters. They had mystical powers and outnumbered the Gaels by four to one.

They had a wicked effigy of a man, made from briars and brooms. It was hollow inside and sometimes it was filled with children and animals which was then set on fire. The Druids believed that burning children would give new life to older Druids. When they sacrificed young animals which would have eaten the herbs of the East, or when they had beheaded an enemy, they would have the head hollowed out. At offertory ceremonies, they would drink from it, in the expectation that it would give them more power.

The Gaels looked on them as barbarous and ferocious. If they did not do as the Druids told them, they would punish them. Their tribes were getting weaker and weaker and they were becoming a downtrodden people. The Druids had spies everywhere and they also had informers. They imprisoned people, at times disfiguring them and then sending them home to their people, who could hardly recognize them as they tried to nurse them back to health. The people regularly asked their leader to lead them in battle, but he knew it would only turn into slaughter.

At last, able to take no more, the chieftain went to his brother in Killeedy and told him of his worries and what was happening in the lands around. He said his forces were getting weaker and that unless they found some way out of their troubles, he would have to find somewhere else in the country for his people to live.

"If I don't," he said, "we will surely be heavily defeated and the survivors will die in slavery. Would you join forces with us? I know that even then, we may not be able to defeat them as their power is very strong. But it would be better to die fighting than to live in slavery."

"What men I have would not improve things," his brother said, "but wait, there is someone I know who could help."

"Tell me who he is," Molicmor asked.

"It is a woman," his brother replied.

"A woman," Molicmor exclaimed, "it's a whole army I want. My good brother, how do you expect a mere woman to help us?"

"Just stop talking and listen," his brother said. "This woman is a princess from beside the river Suir in Waterford. She is a beautiful lady, kind and gentle. She helps those who are in trouble. She especially does not like Druids. She has the power of the living God. She calls Him Jesus. No power can stand against Him. Pick ten of your wisest men and go to visit her."

The chieftain of the Paps Mountains sent ten of his wisest and most cultured men to meet with Ita. They arrived on the hill in Killeedy, Cork on horseback and went straight to meet with Ita. She looked at their horses, one in particular which was a dun colour. She sat on a large stone and listened to them as they dismounted and told her the trouble they were having with the Druids and the cruel things that were happening to their women and children.

"We were at the limit of our endurance," they said, "and could not live with it any longer. Then we heard of your living God, the one called Jesus, He who died and rose again and led them back to the promised land."

"I will teach you some more when your troubles are settled," Ita said, after they had talked for some time. "I will need ten days to put our church and school in safe hands."

She appointed three holy men and had teachers trained for her school. She left on horseback with ten of her holy men and ten of the chieftain's men. In a place now known as Millstreet, the people came out to welcome her. Further on she met a force of Druids, who warned her to turn and ride away, or they would punish the people. She pulled her sword from its sheath.

"This sword is the sword of Jesus Christ," she cried, "the only true God. It shall destroy any power which opposes it. I will confront you at The Paps mountain in the morning."

There the Gaelic men joined with Princess Ita and the fight began. The Druids were able to scatter the princess's men against whom they were throwing rocks, boulders, trees and driving them into the river. But they could not overcome Ita. Every time she swung her sword, some of the Druids died. In turn, Ita's men soon learned that when they stood close to the Princess, they could not be harmed.

Day after day the battle raged on and Ita's men began to regain some of their former fighting ability. They watched her great sword as if receiving inspiration from it. They wondered that whenever men fell from a blow of it, there was never any blood on the sword. The high priests never fought on the field of battle themselves, they just helped by sending out their source of power. They were being driven back slowly but surely towards their headquarters. On the other hand, the Gaels were getting stronger, remembering all the wrongs that had been done to them. Their swords struck as they could see victory within sight. Their weapons fell straight and true, as if by magic or more likely by the hand of God, or by the example of Ita's holy sword.

Then a sevant of the Druids' high priests begged the princess to stop the fighting. Ita raised her sword, put it back in its sheath and the fighting stopped. She had been fasting for two and a half days and had refused even water. One of the high priests stepped out and spoke.

"Most graceful lady, you are a magnificent fighter, Your Gods are powerful. Our great high priest is also a great fighter and he too has a great god. He would like to fight you in single combat. Let you and your God be the combatants."

"So be it," said the Holy Woman, "I will agree if it brings peace to these people." Again Ita withdrew her sword from its sheath and held it up in front of her.

"Wait," said the Druid, "there are rules we have to abide by. If by your ability, you beat our great high priest, we will abandon our gods that we have served through time. On the other hand, it would be only fair, if he defeats you, you will have to obey our high priest and adore our gods."

Ita agreed, in the full knowledge and confidence of the greater power of her God and His ability to defeat any mortal opposition.

The high priest stood at his high altar and waved the instruments of his art, weaving evil spells all day. Ita held up her father's sword, whispered a prayer to Jesus and, it is said, three lights shone from it, one for each of the three members of the Holy Trinity. Now, as the tall ghostly looking high priest of the Druids came from the darkness, light music came from somewhere nearby. His attire comprised of a short tunic, a dark cloak, fastened with a brooch, long lace stockings and pointed shoes. He had a long pointed sword which was red like the colour of blood. He was about six feet six tall and weighed eighteen stone. He looked ancient, like someone from another world.

The fight began between the lovely Celtic maiden and the giant of the British Druids. Slowly at first, they tempted one another to do something rash. Then, they began to move faster, the Druid trying to use his brute strength to break through Ita's defence. But Ita was much more nimble and moved far faster than the Druid warrior. He then tried to show his skill with the sword. It gave the impression that blood dropped from it, but Ita seemed more inspired and looked as if she were indulging herself. Any time he drew blood from her, she in turn drew blood from him, no more no less each. Again her sword never showed blood on it, but it seemed to take on a brightness. The longer she went on, the more courage she showed.

Slowly, the Druid began to take on a confused look. He could not understand why he could not defeat her. He pulled a short cudgel from under his cloak and tried to trap her between the wood and his sword. She now knew where his source of evil power was coming from and found ways to cut it off. She moved from one side to the other to quickly block it.

The Druid seemed to get weaker and more frantic. She moved in closer and with one clear swipe, severed his mighty head from his body.

The Druids and the Gaels stood in amazement, as they looked at the lifeless head. Then the Holy Woman moved again. With her sword, she lifted the giant's head and, with little effort, placed it back on his shoulders and he regained his life, thus showing everyone the power of her God.

The Druid high priest, restored to life, looked different now and more pleasant looking. He gazed at Ita with shining eyes. Although he was six and a half feet tall, he seemed to be looking up at her. "For a few minutes, I was in another world," he said slowly, "and it seemed like eternity. There I saw many great spirits and I know now what these great spirits want me to do."

He went down on his knees and presented her with his sword saying: "Holy Woman, here is my sword, it is a token of the service which I, and my people, offer to you and your living God."

After this battle, the Gaels and the Druids combined. It inspired them to live together as a strong Christian force. After her missionary conquest of the region, Ita established a convent and a church in the area, giving Christians a strong hand. The convent in Kilmeady became prosperous and a centre of knowledge and learning for her followers.

Battle of Cullen

A message came from the Druids in Millstreet who had not been converted to Christianity by the Holy Woman, Ita. Since the day she had converted many of their number, their unconverted companions had sought every help to get rid of her by fair means or foul. They could see her getting stronger every day and it made it even more difficult and bitter to see their own high priest working in Ita's church with so many of his followers. They sent for reinforcements to Peakeen Mountain, near Kenmare, where the Druids were a strong force, and the High Priest there assembled a force of five hundred and fifty men, including some Gaels over which they had influence. They told the fighting men that the witch Ita had great power and that if she was not destroyed she would take over the whole countryside. She would bring evil to everyone.

CULLEN BATTLE SITE

The plan was that they should descend on Ita and her followers when least expected and wipe them out and take over their territory. When the men who had gone with her would see that she had been beaten, they would return to their own side and fight with them. They travelled mostly by night so that they would have the element of surprise on this witch. Soon, they thought, the Druids in Millstreet would regain their former glory and, once more, be the masters of the Gaels.

Then, early one morning, Jesus appeared to Ita, telling her that her enemies were coming for her once again. They had a strong force ranged against her, she was told, and she should leave Millstreet and bring the element of surprise with her to a place called Cullen.

The princess was able to put together three hundred and twenty five men including the Druid and his companions, who was now a great defender of the Holy Woman. They moved off for Cullen early on a Tuesday evening. They camped in a grove under the hill and watched for the arrival of the Druids' army from Kenmare.

Later that night, the Kenmare men moved in and camped near the river, never knowing what or who was waiting for them. They lit small fires to cook food, but otherwise, they kept quiet.

Ita's men rested, preparing for a silent and surprise assault on the Druids of Kenmare. As soon as dawn was breaking, her forces made a sudden attack. The Kenmare men were greatly surprised and, although they made feeble efforts, they could not react quickly enough. Because of the surprise nature of the attack, the battle was soon over.

The former Druid priest showed he still had plenty of fighting ability and in two hours the battle was won and a truce made. There should be no more fighting, they agreed. The high priest leader of the defeated Kenmare men stood in dismay and, looking up, saw his former colleague from Millstreet. He looked at the former Druid in disgust, lost all reason and in two long jumps, he was upon him, to strike a deadly blow. Ita's man somehow dodged the assault and managed to draw his sword.

A titanic battle between the two men followed. The power of their swords could be felt as they moved up and down. Now one retreated, then the other was pinned to the ground and not a word was spoken between them and no sound was heard except the clash of their swords and their heavy breathing. It would be a fight to the finish, up and down the hill of Cullen. They fought along the bank of the river, where the dead and wounded lay. The weak and injured watched in amazement, waiting for one or the other to get tired or make a fatal mistake.

After an hour of savage fighting there was still no victor. Now one slipped and fell into the swift flowing waters of the river, to be followed by the other. There they stood, with the waters flowing around them. Although they were large men, the water was still up to their waists. They moved forward and backwards in turn with the crowd watching them from the riverbank, waiting for the contest to end.

The crowd cheered their leaders on and, as the Milstreet man pushed his opponent back, his foot snagged on something in the river bed, falling backwards into the strong current. He still had his hand above water, however, still clutching the sword. Ita's man moved quickly and, with one swing of the sword, he cut off the Kenmare man's hand just above the wrist. In dismay, his followers watched the hand, still carrying the sword, float down the river.

The Druid was helped out of the river and had to stand in front of the saint. She rebuked him for breaking the truce, saying it was a cross he would have to carry for the rest of his life. He begged for Ita's forgiveness saying, that like his colleague, he would serve her God for the rest of his life. Then most of the Druids that had been spared decided to follow Ita. Those few who did not opt to become Christians, left quickly and in some disarray.

They were curious about her and fascinated with every word she spoke. They discussed her message among themselves and could see she was a very devout person.

Ita walked around among the people for several days and spoke to the fighters, attending to their wounds, talking about the living God, telling them that He did not want them to fight with one another. He did not want them to worship false gods, she told them, but wanted them to love one another, whether they were from Cork, Clare or Kenmare. They were all brothers and God wanted them to live in harmony and do His will.

Without knowing fully what Ita meant, their leader, sat and thought to himself. Then he suddenly stood up and looked around at his people who were standing around the field and by the river, saying 'I committed a great offence against this Holy Woman, by breaking my word of honour. We the Druids had evil powers causing evil things to happen. Now I have a feeling of great joy and excitement at what this gracious woman tells us. I am still struggling to grasp the significance of what we are learning here today. One thing I know, this new knowledge is for the good of our people. You have trusted me in the past and I ask you to trust me now and trust this True and Living God. I now invite Ita to baptise us in this little spring around which we are standing.'

Now Ita seemed to be Mother of all and she was sure she was doing the work of God. With a stick in one hand and a small container in the other, she asked if they consented with a free will to become children of God. She baptized each one as they confessed their sins. 'I prepare you for the way of the Lord', she would tell them. 'The crooked shall be made smooth; all flesh shall see the salvation of God. I baptise thee with this holy water, which God has provided for us. Holy, Holy, Holy Trinity; Father, Son, Holy Spirit, Amen'.

The high priest, leader of the Kenmare men went with her to Millstreet, then on to Killeedy in Limerick to learn the ways of God. In time, he became a Holy Man and wished to come back to Cullen to build a church and school for Ita. Despite the loss of his hand, he looked after the Cullen people for many years and led a life of great purity. The memory of this saint has been preserved with great veneration.

The Three Sisters Wells

Slánan, Slan, Ann, Saint Ita's well is built in the shape of a horseshoe as it was the animal that the saint loved best. Her well was built by the Druid who became a holy man. He was a mason and he also made a holy water font for the saint. It still survives and once stood on the left hand side of the entrance to the Holy Woman's church. It was the first act a skilled Druid mason had done for a church in Ireland.

Ita was so pleased, she immediately filled it with water and a large crowd gathered for prayers. Everybody was impressed and

Original Water Font at Kilmeady, Millstreet

she asked him to continue and build a church. He had many volunteers to help him and they worked late in the evenings and early in the mornings. The walls were built in one month and it was roofed and completed in seven weeks. It was forty feet long and twenty feet wide. Its foundations can still be traced quite clearly and stones from Ita's church are strewn all over the ancient graveyard. Some of the stones were used to build the tombs at a later stage and others were made into gravestones.

Tubrid, Well of Ita

Near the Clara mountains, Ita fought her first, greatest and fiercest battle against the ferocious Druids, her first battle with her holy sword. While she fought, a glow came from her and her sword and the Druids greatly feared, and with good reason, her sword and her God. For the rest of the day after the fighting ended, she moved around healing men as well as women and children. The spring from which she took water was a small one, with barely enough to drink. Ita told the people they would have more water the next day and, sure enough, the following morning everybody was amazed as the flow of water had increased over a hundred fold or more. And so started one of the biggest of the wells associated with Ita.

Slán Well at Kilmeady, Millstreet

Tubrid Holy Well, Millstreet

St. Ita's Well at Cullen,
Kilmeady

Slán Well Kilmeady

Slán Well, or St. Ita's Well in Kilmeady has been for centuries, a place of great veneration and remains so even to the present day. Elderly people had great faith in its healing powers and often told stories that had been handed down through the years, of favours which had been granted there. One such story tells of a little girl who could not walk and was cured by the blessed waters.

The well is situated in a field about 200 yards to the right of the main road on the approach to Kilmeady Bridge from the Millstreet direction. It is one of a number of interesting features which make up this historical location. Beside it stands the tomb in which are buried the chieftains of Mount Leader's estate. It is encased by a stone-built protecting outer wall, with iron railings on top. The waters of the Holy Well leave by a stream flowing into the Fionn Abha. It is customary to walk around Ita's well, praying all the time and children are carried on their parent's back. This is the favoured way in which to seek, and possibly to be granted, healing.

The following prayers are recited: Five Our Fathers, Five Hail Marys and Five Glorias. It is said that St. Ita baptized many babies there, some of whom were in poor health from the undernourishment of their mothers. After baptism the babies' health improved and so the well was known as Tobar Slán. Offerings are usually laid there in thanksgiving for favours granted. The well itself is built roughly in the shape of a horse shoe, a work of great art, built with a loving hand.

The site of St. Ita's church is still visible in an ancient graveyard, emphasizing Divine activity back to the early days of Christian teaching. It is easy to be transported back to the time of St. Ita and time seems to stand still, untouched by the passing centuries.

There is beauty in the old trees in all their shapes and sizes, each of their boughs and branches telling its own story. The stones are in various forms with no names but, for those who would look for it, there is a sense of the presence of those warrior spirits who fought St. Ita's battles in the true and certain knowledge that they were fighting for what was right and that they had Divine help through the intercession of the Holy Woman herself.

While at Tobar Slán, it is possible to experience the closeness of God and, when leaving, to take nothing away, leaving behind worries, sickness and troubles of everyday life. God is there to solve those problems and peace and tranquility can be found at Tobar Slán. St. Ita proved to be a valiant champion for the Christian cause, by leading her followers in true Celtic fashion. She led them to victory over the Druids from Britain who had occupied the lands known as West Muskerry in Cluden, Millstreet. It was there she established a convent and a school for girls, which later took in boys and she renamed the region Kilmeady after her church and convent. Ita also trained many teachers, that they might spread the Christian faith and free the people from the slavery of ignorance.

Many exciting things happened in this era of new life. In the name of Jesus, bridges of community love were built between the different tribes who previously had been bitter enemies. The children of the various tribes, the Druids and the people of the Kilmeady area sent their children to St. Ita's school. Though they began their education as pagans, many were converted to the True Faith during this time. They later became Ita's apostles for the evangelisation of the district. These apostles or missionaries, along with Ita moved around among the people, preaching the true faith, leaving them as a strong and unified community which they continue to be to this day.

St. Ita's graveyard is full of stones, scattered all over the site. Some are headstones, while others are from the church of which only the foundations are visible now. Also to be seen is a big holy water font made of stone. It once stood at the door of her church. It was carved from a large stone by one of the leaders of the Druids, who was a mason. For this, Ita gave him the honour of being the first person to be baptised in the church. The building measured forty feet by twenty feet, had a twenty foot high stone wall and a thatch roof, with a door is on the east side.

Battle of Killeedy

Before Ita was known in Killeedy, Limerick Chief Corcu Oche, the leader of all the Hy Connail people was threatened by several chiefs of west Munster. They said they would combine forces to wipe out the Chief and his people, divide their land between themselves and burn their crops and their mud huts. Corcu Oche had only one hundred and forty five men compared to a combined force of four hundred well armed and trained warriors on the enemy side.

It could not be an even fight as Corcu and his men had got few proper fighting weapons. The very young and the older men had only farm implements, as what few proper weapons they had they left to the able bodied men. The boys had little time for instruction in the ways of battle, but they still learned how to swing awkward weapons. Their brave chieftain called everybody together including the women and children.

"My friends," he said, "you are a great people. I want you to know your fate. Unless there is some unknown intervention, we will all be lost when the battle is over. We, your menfolk are willing to die, but what about the rest. Our women will be raped and our children made into slaves. Can anybody suggest anything? Can anybody tell us some way to escape those ruthless, merciless people?"

The crowd all started to talk at once and, as the babble went on, a mature man who had travelled the countryside asked everyone to stop talking and allow him speak.

"In my travels I heard of a beautiful princess," he said. "She is said to come from near a river called the Suir in Waterford. She has great powers and teaches about a living God. She has beaten the Druids in different battles and to anyone who looks for her help, she gives it willingly. She is very kind and gentle. She has a wonderful sword and can stay fighting for days. After the battle is over, she tends to everyone, whether friend or foe."

"I wish such a person existed," said Chief Corcu Oche. It is difficult to believe that a mere woman can do this, but we have nothing to lose. Where can she be found?"

Drawing of St. Ita's Church at Killeedy, Co. Limerick

Graveyard at Killeedy, Co. Limerick

St. Ita's Well at Killeedy, Co. Limerick.

"Not far away," the man replied. "She is in Kilmeady near Millstreet, just two days ride away."

Five men were picked to go and find her and they rode into Millstreet, straight up to Ita's school. On seeing them and how desperate they looked, she immediately closed the school and greeted them warmly. They told her their sad tale of how they and their people were doomed. They begged her to come with them.

"I will give you my answer in the morning," she said, and left some of her holy men in charge and teachers who could look after her school.

Early next morning, she came back to the men and said she was willing and ready to go. They left without delay and made good time as Ita was as experienced a horsewoman as any man. When they arrived at their destination, all the community came out to welcome her. Even the beasts of the field seemed to sense her coming. News of the big force which was on its way to attack them also arrived and she knew they had only about eight hours to prepare for the battle.

She taught the people how to pray and repent for their misdeeds. Then she herself went in solitude to commune with the One, True God on whom she depended so much. She was fearful for what lay ahead.

"Holy Trinity, Father, Son and Holy Spirit," she prayed, "come to the aid of these people and defend them from those fiery Munster hosts. These people are outnumbered, four hundred against one hundred and forty five and have called me to their aid."

After hours of prayer, Ita fell asleep and then Jesus came to her, saying:

"Do not be afraid, my daughter, we have much more work for you to do. Tomorrow will be a good day."

Ita went confidently to the battlefield. Now she could conceive what would happen. She led the tiny army, her sword drawn. She knelt down fourteen yards in front of her men with her sword held high. The west Munster men rushed past her hardly seeing the Holy Woman. They could not wait to wipe out the men of Hy Connail. How easy it would be. When they were close and could look into the eyes of their opponents, they saw their determination for their swords shone brightly.

The first of the west Munster men pulled their weapons out, but they could not wound their opponents. They stood in awe. On the other hand, the tiny army of Hy Conaill saw what was happening. They had nothing to lose and began to fight, mowing the enemy down before them. It was slaughter. Even the boys with the farm implements were doing their part and before long, the enemy warriors were strewn all over the field.

The west Munster men now realised that Ita was their leader and begged her for mercy. The saint raised her holy sword and straight away the conflict ended. Only one of the Hy Connail men had been wounded. They got orders to look after the enemy wounded, ensuring they were all attended to. They had been reduced to just forty five and they were a sorry sight.

Chief Corcu Oche returned from the battlefield, full of gratitude to their new found friends, Ita and her Living God. Jesus was on all their lips. Ita had asked them to do penance before going to battle and to give thanks to God if they obtained victory. One among them did not fulfil his pledge of gratitude and Ita asked for him to be brought to her presence.

According to legend, the man was found to have been wounded during the battle as he had been fighting in the foremost ranks. He was received kindly by the holy virgin who healed his wounds. Through her intercession, he afterwards brought forth fruits of worthy penance. The west Munster people asked to be allowed to stay among the people whom they had come to conquer. They made the Hy Connail army into a sizeable one and were feared far and wide. They were left in peace for a long time. Together they built a church and school for the virgin in Killeedy and there she made her quarters from where she carried out her missionary work throughout Munster.

Kilmeedy, Limerick

In what is now known as Kilmeedy in Co. Limerick, there lived a mighty chieftain called Eochuidh Capail. His lands were fertile and densely populated and he had a strong force of fighters. He was seldom interfered with and when Ita visited his lands, his people came and listened to what she had to say. They began to talk about her and her God and it worried the mighty chief.

He called his trusted men around him to consult with them about what should be done about her. After long discussions and arguments about possible solutions, it was decided she should be driven out before she could get too strong. He wanted to know all about her and heard that she was a princess, the daughter of a Decies King. She had no fear, he was told, and could lead men into battle. Her sword had been given to her by her God. She cured people who were ill or dying, they informed him, but he rejected it all and said that they would call her bluff. He, the chieftain was seldom beaten.

The Parish Church of St. Ita in Kilmeedy, Limerick

The plan was first to start skirmishing to show their prowess at fighting and maybe then she would leave and allow him to rule his land. As she was a princess, she should know he would not stand for any nonsense. These battles went on for some time, until Itaís men were wounded and she decided she would have to pay this war lord a visit. She and a modest force of forty men rode into the fort.

Eochuidh Capail did not receive her with courtesy and he did not ask her to dismount. He told her she should go immediately or else he would kill her and her warriors. Neither his grandfather nor his father had ever lost a battle and he was not about to lose one now. If she would leave straight away, he told her, he would not harm her as he was a quiet and peaceful man.

Gate of the Cemetery in Kilmeady, Co. Limerick

Ita calmly told him that she had beaten armies throughout Munster with ten times as big a force as he had; some of them evil and violent. If he would not leave them in peace, she would turn her powerful God on him, much as she would dislike doing it. She and her men dismounted, their hands not far from their swords.

The chief's wife ran towards him saying 'My lord, soon our only son will be dead, while you stand here in our time of need, arguing with a strange woman'.

His face turned pale as if the blood had drained from it and his shoulders slouched as if a mighty weight had been laid on them. Their son, a young talented rider, barely eleven years old, had once too often attempted to ride a high spirited wild young horse. He threw his young rider, then charged him with his front leg and opened a large wound in the crown of the boy's head. He had been carried in to his beehive abode and there he lay lifeless for months. His poor mother's heart was sorely tried and even with healing Druids and other healers coming to him, he still lay lifeless except for an occasional low groan.

His father realised that now that the final parting was about to happen, he would not have a son to carry on his family line, or to carry on the fighting ability which he, his father, his grandfather and his ancestors had had, going back for generations. His line would end with him.

Now, this strange woman was looking at him and he seemed dazed and bewildered. Ita laid her hand softly on him.

"Do not despair," she said, "our God is good. I will go and see what can be done". She left the crowd with determination and went to where the dying boy lay. She stayed with him for several hours while a large crowd waited in the cold. She beseeched God to come to her aid once again. Now in expectation and excitement, they looked at Ita and the boy. He moved on his bed and then rose to his feet, appearing to be fully restored to health.

Ita was hailed as if she herself were some kind of a God and the boy was hugged by his mother and father, asking them about the white horse. His father said he would have to be destroyed.

"No," said Ita firmly, "you do not have to do that."

Kilmeedy, Limerick with the foundations of St. Ita's original Church

Site of St. Ita's ancient Church, Kilmeedy, Co. Limerick.

"Will you take charge of him, Lady," asked the Chief and Ita replied that she would be pleased to do as he asked. In days to come, the horse would become her favourite and be with her in many battles and trials. Now the chieftain asked her to speak about her God to his people.

'It is a great honour for me to be among you, my dear people,'she told the assembled village, "I am but the handmaid of my God. It was not I who healed the boy. It is Jesus, the Son of the living God who is the healer. He cures not only his friends, but lepers, the blind, the crippled, the abandoned, as well as widows and children. His love and His power can overcome evil. Jesus has both Divine nature and human nature. God is our loving father who looks after us all, just as a good father looks after his children."

When Ita had finished her talk, the chieftain asked her if there was anything else she wished for. 'Yes' said Ita 'I want you and your people to come to Killeedy to be baptized.'

"No, No," said the proud Chieftain. "We will not go to Killeedy. We will build our own church here. You must come to us, to our church, to the Church of Jesus.

"Yes," said Ita, smiling, "it will be as you wish." And so was built Ita's church in Kilmeady and it was completed in six months. The ruins are still there together with the graveyard and is identified with St. Ita's name on the gate.

Ita's
Parish
Church,
Feenagh,
Kilmeedy,
Limerick

Princess Eannaigh

Princess Eanneaigh left Kilmeaden and travelled to Kilmeady, near Millstreet, County Cork to her sister Ita, accompanied by four horsemen. She was not as good a horsewoman as her sister and, in consequence, they had to make stops on the way at Fermoy, Kilcolman and Rathluirc. Late in the evening of the third day they reached Millstreet to find the gates of Ita's compound closed. Men were heard shouting outside and those inside, with the exception of Ita, were fearful of an invasion.

Weather's Well where St. Brendan was Baptised

"What do you mean by disturbing the house of God at this hour of the night," she called to the travelers and then came a shock of joy for they were indeed her own people, men from the Decies.

"The Lady Eanneaigh is with us, wanting to see her sister," they answered and the gates were opened. Ita ran to meet her sister as she dismounted from her horse. Not until now did she realise how much she had missed her and the rest of her family since she had left her own countryside. She looked into her sister's eyes, unable to speak. Eanneaigh had grown to womanhood but still had not changed.

"What brings you here, my dear sister," Ita asked.

"I made myself a promise I would follow you some day," was Eanneaigh's simple reply, "and here I am."

After the three day ride, Eannaigh was saddle-sore and tired. With tears in their eyes the sisters could not stop talking, love pouring from one to the other.

"Tell me what happened on your journey here," asked Eanneaigh.

"I will tell you nothing until you have eaten," replied Ita. When food had been provided for the visitor, Ita watched while her sister ate, asking few questions. She longed to know what news there was from the Decies, but she must wait, for Eanneaigh was worn out by the journey and the excitement of their reunion. The young woman put down her spoon and Ita took her to her cell. Afterwards, Eanneaigh could hardly recall her crossing the fort and being helped to prepare for bed by her sister.

When Ita returned the next day, Eannaigh awoke tired and still saddle sore. She lay on her simple bed, gradually becoming conscious of the sheepskin wrapped around her. Once more she fell asleep and, an hour later she opened her eyes to see Ita fondly gazing into her eyes.

"Can I stay with you," Eannaigh asked Ita anxiously.

"I am sure Jesus had a purpose in sending you here," Ita answered "It will be a new start for us both. Our mother must have been lonely when you left?"

"She gives all her time doting on Nessa," said Eannaigh.

"Nessa! Who is Nessa?," Ita asked, curiosity rising within her.

"Surely you got word of our new sister, Nessa," replied Eannaigh.

"No I did not," said Ita, "tell me all about her. What is she like?"

"She is fair and very solemn like you in some ways."

They chatted on about their loving father who had died in Clashmore; her dear uncle who died defending her in Gortroe; her evil uncle who sought to sell her to their enemy and lost his life to the Druids. So many had died needlessly, so many of their warriors, all good men. It had to be God's will, for Jesus was always there for her in times of danger.

"He will always be there for you too Eanneaigh," she finished aloud and she suddenly realised she no longer wanted to ask the hundred questions that had crowded her mind. God had sent her sister to her for some good reason.

Later, they would go out on their rounds, two princesses in their own right, working for God in different ways. Ita worked for the spiritual good of the people, Eanneaigh for their physical and material welfare.

After some time, a request came from Limerick for Ita to go there, as some people needed her help. They got word that the Chief's brother in Mount Collins had been badly wounded while out hunting deer. His horse had fallen on ragged rocks and was killed, leaving his rider severely injured and fighting for his life. By now, Eanneaigh had a reputation of her own for curing the sick, which Ita encouraged.

They both went to the fort, to the sick man's bedside. They prayed over him, invoking the Blessed Trinity to restore him to health. After four hours or more, Ita told her sister he would recover, but to continue nursing him. She had a purpose in this. It was believed by the chief and his people that it was Eanneaigh who healed the wounded man and they claimed she had worked a miracle.

Ita's permission was sought to build a small church in honour of Eanneaigh and she granted their request. This was where Ita baptised the people from the surrounding area. A well sprang up

Killenagh Well

close by, which is still known as Cill Eanneaigh Holy Well and is venerated to this day.

Eannaigh went out at dawn each day making good use of her nursing skills. She often had to deal with epidemics and diseases which caused the deaths of many. Her work was often described as mystical. She trained young girls as nurses and they served the people all over Munster. She was a beautiful woman and often, as she travelled through the countryside, she was made offers of marriage. She refused them all gracefully and it never seemed to cause any strife among the men, until one day two stepsons of a chieftain were talking of Eannaigh's beauty. One brother said he dared to ask for the princess's hand in marriage. The elder brother angrily said 'How dare you, that was my privilege as the elder' and they started to wrestle over who had the greater right. The younger brother fell eight feet off a cliff and was so severely injured that he was in danger of death.

The chieftain knew he had to get Eannaigh's help and he sent out several messengers to find her. She was located over the next mountain, teaching the people there new skills. She hastened to the sick man's bedside and proceeded to treat him with her herbal medicines. She had learned all about them as a young girl on the banks of the river Suir. She also prayed for two days and three nights. Slowly but surely the young man recovered. When his father sought the Angel of Mercy Eannaigh, she was not to be found. Nobody knew where she had gone. She was responding to one of the many calls which were waiting for her and which she readily and willingly answered, leaving the chieftain and his people to get on with their daily lives.

*   *   *

A messenger came to Eannaigh with an account of a mother of a large family who was giving birth to another baby. The local woman was not able to deliver the baby properly. The mother and baby would be lost without Eannaigh's experienced hands. The evening was cold, wet and windy as she headed towards Mount Brandon. She arrived late in the afternoon, cold and wet through to the skin. After some time, her skillful hands delivered the baby. The mother needed further nursing as her life was still in danger. By morning, Eannaigh was able to leave on another call, still wearing her wet cloak. After some distance she began feeling sick and weak. She began to stumble and fall and, luckily, there were some kind people nearby who saw her plight and took her to their home. She had developed pneumonia and became progressively more ill. After getting weaker and weaker, in three days she had died. Holy men and women came from all parts of Munster for her burial and many noble families arrived from all parts of Ireland. Her sister's sorrow was the greatest and Ita wondered what she would do without the support of Eanneaigh in the future. Those among whom she had worked could not believe that she was no longer among them and mourned her loss.

Eannaigh died in or about the year 525 aged 51 years. Interment took place at Tobraid, which is to be found near Ardfert on the road towards Abbeydorney. This is near to the place where Brendan was baptized. There is a small rectangular enclosure around her grave, with a mound to the eastern side. The grave looks so fresh, it is difficult to believe that she has been so long buried. She was interred there on the 1st May, (Bealtaine), the month of Mary, Our Mother, on whose life she modelled hers.

Ita buried her sister Eannaigh near Brendan's Well at Ardfert, creating another tie between these three great Saints of post-Patrician Ireland.

Brendan, A Mhic

In the Celtic period, children were given as foster children from one Chieftain to another. When a Chieftain had no children of his own, foster children cemented a bond between one royal household and another. When Christianity came, they discontinued this practice and brought their first-born son to Ita and to God to be fostered. Not only had she to be mother, guardian and teacher, she had to have practical common-sense. It is because of this Irish custom of fostering that Ita, the Virgin of Christ takes on a special character and poignancy which is lacking in the life of other saints.

She devoted herself to teaching the young, and when the youths came to Ita, few of them could read or write. Part of the Celtic culture was to memorise poems and stories, for that is how such works were handed down from one generation to another.

"And truth which has only been written on leaves or on sand,
Has stayed among us in the songs of our land."

The first of Ita's foster children was also one of the most famous. His name is regularly on the lips of Irish people almost two millennia after his great exploits and his deeds are told and retold the world over.

St. Brendan was born in 504, a Kerryman of royal blood. The new religion called Christianity appealed to his family. His father Finnlugh was of the old Irish tribe of Cian and his beautiful mother's name was Cara. Their child was born near Tralee and it was decided he should be named Braen-Finn, the Bright Drop. Breanoinn, as the name became known, or later again Brendan, having been brought up by his parents for six years at home, was made ready for formal education. Erc the holy man was sent for. As a young man and Bishop of Altraighe Caille, Erc had been the first of Laoghaire's Brehons to acknowledge Patrick. In old age he would be among the first of the southern prelates to befriend the young Holy Woman who had settled in Cluain Credail. Now, he took Brendan to the Virgin Ita when she first came to Limerick.

Erc arrived with seven of his men on horseback and, when Ita saw him approaching, she wondered if it was old Simeon, stepping out from the pages of St. Luke's gospel and holding in his arms the Light of the World. Instead, it was Bishop Erc holding a young boy in his arms.

He rode up to Ita and spoke sharply and without preamble.

"I have brought you your first foster-son," he told her abruptly. "This is Brendan, the child of Cara and Finnlugh, a noble couple belonging to the people of Ciarraight Luachra. He is their first-born, so they have offered him to God. You will keep him here, my girl, until he is old enough to begin studies with me. Teach him all you can."

He left no room for dissent and he mounted his horse and rode off with his men again.

Ita took the child into her arms, too astonished to make any reply. She had planned for herself a life of contemplation and solitude, of fixed hours for the singing of psalms, for study and for work, a life whose sacred horarium would not be interrupted by anything in creation. Now, she knew instinctively that God, Who had denied her fasting, would also take from her, her hours of silent meditation. He would accept the myrrh of mortification and the incense of prayer so neatly laid aside for Him. He would sweep it all away and take nothing but her work.

For her part, Ita would accept what He gave her, like the gift of this small child. He was the first foster child that God had given to her and Ita knew he would be only one of many.

Now, as she looked down at him, the child was warm in her arms, and she had no choice but to care for him. Erc returned the following day to his hermitage and perhaps as he went, he reflected a moment on the usefulness of women, or perhaps he never gave them a thought. When he was gone, Ita stood once more on a road that she had not chosen to go.

First the little boy cried for his mother and father as he had been taken from them abruptly and he missed them deeply. Day and night Ita kept Brendan with her. He slept in her cell and she always fed him with fresh warm milk from the cow. He lay out in the sunshine while she worked nearby, sewing or knitting. There was never a half-hour when she felt free of him. When he would wander off, she would have to protect him from the road, the river and the cattle. As a normal, active child, he got up to every mischief he could. He would hide and she would not be able to find him.

As a result of their closeness through those early years, Brendan would carry the voice of his foster mother with him wherever he sailed through the world. He would remember the many times she blessed the food and said grace after meals in her low, deep voice.

Brendan sat with Ita one day under a hawthorn tree, trying to read some words she had written for him.

"My soul thirsts for Thee," he recited slowly and without expression, as he tried to read from Scripture.

"Mother," he asked, "what is this thirsty for Thee? Can you drink God?"

"We can, a mhic," she replied, "I drank Him this morning. He looked like wine."

"I want to drink Him too," said the small boy.

"Tell Him that you want Him," said Ita, "there are not many who tell Him that they want Him." The boy shut his eyes to make his prayer without distraction, while his foster mother looked at his pale face with the princely features. As she watched him, he opened his eyes.

"I told Him," he said to Ita, "did he hear me?"

"He heard you as I hear you now, only more clearly" Ita told the boy.

"What does God look like?" he asked.

"I cannot tell you what He looks like," said Ita, "but I remember when I was a child, dreaming on the banks of the Suir, I saw three jewels and a voice told me that it was the Father, Son and Holy Spirit whom I saw living in my soul."

Brendan's Question

Brendan of Clonfert, with whom St. Ita had a very close friendship, had asked her which three works were most pleasing to God's sight. The spouse of Christ answered easily.

"Confident resignation of a pure heart to God; a simple religious life and magnanimity with charity. These three works are most agreeable to the Lord." Whereupon she was asked which three things were most displeasing to God. St. Ita was again able to reply without hesitation.

"A countenance hating men; affection of depravity in the heart; an absorbing love of riches. These are the three things which are very displeasing in God's sight."

Brendan and those who were present admired the holy virginís wisdom and they gave praise to God, who appeared to have spoken through the lips of His gifted servant. The saint was accustomed to retire frequently into some secret place, where she gave herself up entirely to prayer and Divine contemplation; especially revolving in her mind the mysteries of the Holy Trinity, which nearly always formed the subject of her sublime meditations, and which excited devotional fervour within her soul.

Anxious to behold her during these moments of transport and rapt adoration, a holy virgin stole upon her unawares, and beheld three brilliant globes of light, radiant as the sun. These shed an intense and a lustrous glare over the whole space surrounding her. Alarmed at this vision, the virgin felt unable to approach Ita. She returned, however, filled with admiration at this unexpected apparition, emblematic of the usual subject matter occupying our saintís contemplative aspirations.

*   *   *   *   *

A few years passed in this way while first one, then another of those Christian families of Munster brought their sons to Ita for fostering at a very early age. Ita found herself surrounded by a nursery full of very young boys, She knew now that she could never return to the solitary life she once planned for herself and she no longer wanted to. She could see and understand what God had planned for her and she knew now she would have to have more knowledge if her foster sons were to travel to distant parts of the world, to spread the Word of God. She had a working knowledge of Latin, Greek, Hebrew and Mathematics and she would work to improve them and pass them on to those in her care. Brendan studied and steadily advanced in these subjects, as well as in Geography, Sacred Scriptures and Astronomy, a subject that was to come in very useful to him one day.

The great Ita, Virgin and Holy Woman taught him many things, but most of all she taught him to love God, to develop a knowledge and love of the sea, the reading of the stars, what Irish courage meant and how to conquer. When Ita had taught him all she had to give, he was approaching twelve years of age and she sent him to Erc.

*　　　　*　　　　*　　　　*　　　　*

With every settlement and Convent which Ita set up throughout Munster, she was given as much land as she needed for her good work with the poor and many converts. God saw to it that she had an abundance of crops and she cultivated vegetables widely which helped her to instruct the women of the day in the best forms of food and eating habits.

Ita raised cattle, sheep, goats and poultry and the people made their own cheese and butter and picked wild berries for jam making. They fertilized the crops and reseeded them to grow new harvests. Small rivers were turned onto the land to improve the crops and all this gave a living to the people around. The women ground the grain by pushing heavy implements across a flat stone and many of Ita's practical ways gave the people back their dignity. Amid all of this, a great sense of happiness was evident. Stone axes of various sizes were used to cut down trees and antler picks were used for hoeing the ground. Small implements such as bone needles had many uses in the domestic life of that time. People learned how to polish the rough stone tools to make them more effective. Those polished tools were used to hollow out tree trunks to make boats or simple wooden stools and seats.

Ita and her people lived a simple, carefree life with music, singing, dancing and folklore being widely cultivated. They were very proud of their culture which had been handed down to them through many generations.

St. Ita's Great Fasts

Often the Collect of a saint's Mass underlines one or two of their characteristic virtues. St. Ita's speaks instead of her 'innumerable gifts' and it seems, indeed, that from the beginning of her religious life people were won by every aspect of her pleasing personality, while at the same time they were moved by her innocence of life.

But many Catholic women have reached maturity with the endowments Íta then had, charm, intelligence, piety and yet, very few have become acknowledged saints. We see this when, in modern Irish life, a Catholic mother refuses the Church the son or daughter whom God has chosen for Himself. We see it too, when such a woman makes a division between the husband and bride whom God Himself has joined together.

What is lacking? It might be generosity, it might be insight that at least lets us see what we should be giving, so that when we hold it back we are ashamed. It might be the habit of looking to God from hour to hour for guidance, travelling uncomfortably through life, yet going in the right direction, not letting middle or old age overtake us, keeping us in a rut of our own making. Whatever this indefinable quality may be, King Kennfoelad's daughter had it, and used it to great effect.

There is an incident in the early religious life of Ita that brings out clearly both her generosity and her ability to accept God's guidance, even though it meant stepping from the path that she had determined to follow.

During her first months as Abbess, Ita's fasts had become longer and more frequent. Two, three or even four days might be spent without a mouthful of bread to strengthen her. Her companions may not have realised that her health was at risk as a result and would break if she continued fasting. Even if they had, they may have found her unimpressed by any advice they might offer. But considering the spirit of the age in which they lived, the more probable explanation is that they looked on her abstinence as miraculous, and only wished that they themselves could subsist on two meals a week.

So for a time the young Abbess continued undisturbed, her enjoyment - and abuse - of her late won independence. She had given ample proof of her generosity; now God would test her submission.

One evening, after a fast of three days, Ita rested in her cell, too weary to unfold her needlework and hoping only for strength enough to cross to the Chapel at nightfall. It was summer time and the cell was half-filled with light from the doorway.

A young man appeared at the threshold. Through dim, startled eyes, Ita saw that his 'brat' and tunic were white and his face stern. It was not the first time that an angel had visited a virgin, but this angel had not come to proclaim her full of grace.

"Your fasts are excessive," he began, "your penance is exaggerated."

Tears of sheer terror slid down Ita's cheeks.

"Bride of Christ," he continued more gently, "it is sin you must extinguish, not nature."

"But I have set my heart on going forward," Ita replied, "do not ask me to turn back." So dependence would be no small sacrifice to ask of her, one who was ready to argue with an angel, a messenger from the very God to whom she had dedicated her life.

More tears slid down her cheeks, but this time they sprang from disappointment. She had so wanted to prove her love of Christ and now this angel would not let her. Must she walk then with the mediocre? Was she to lead a life no more ordinary than that which she had left in her home in the Decies, with the music, the banqueting, the bright colours, so dear to the heart of a Celt? She was ready to give all to find all, but she had not wrested herself from the arms of those who loved her, in order to lead a life of commonplace virtue, to eat bread and butter with the common of the faithful. She had thought that in selling all, she would find the pearl of great price; now it seemed that even the pearl was not to be hers. She would be queen neither in this world nor in the next.

Such thoughts as these passed through her mind. She did not understand the order transmitted to her by the Angel who still stood before her. Perhaps to the end of her life, something in her would rebel against the care she had to give herself, and yet, without her mind's consent, the soul obeyed. If God would have her eat, drink and rest, let it be so; she did not understand, but let it be so.

The great Angel had stood watching her, waiting for her consent; then he knelt close to where she lay.

"God loves you," he told her, "and so tenderly that He Himself has sent you bread from Heaven." So He did love her, she thought to herself. He had not counted her worthy to share His desert hunger or His Calvary thirst, but He loved her. The Angel went to Ita's writing table where he cut a slice from a loaf he had brought. He spread it with honey, then gave it to her and watched her eat. He poured out some milk and lifted the drink to her lips.

"What is your name?" she asked

"My name is Mithiden," he replied. "I am the angel sent to you on the day you left your Mother's womb. Since then I have been the guardian of your purity; jealously have I cherished it for the pleasure of my Lord. I have watched your thoughts, I have guided them towards Him and what I could not touch - your power of will - there I have prayed on your behalf and ceased not until I saw it swing towards Him whom I serve. Nor will I leave you, radiant woman, until I have led you into the house of the Great King, your Spouse."

Ita knelt there long after he had gone. Her eyes closed against the sunlight that still streamed in. She drew close to God and, facing Him in prayer, she knew for the first time that sense of unexpected peace and freedom with which God rewards those who are ready, for His sake, to submit their judgment, to admit they have been wrong. An incident which follows on this, shows how, during the months between, her mind had worked on the lesson of the loaf. She would always be ascetic, but she would not again confuse fasting with charity.

St. Brendan

St. Ita

St. Brendan
Nenagh

St. Ita
Clonea Power

St. Ita, U.C.C.
Honan Chapel

St. Ita
Nenagh

St. Ita
Kilgobinet

St. Ita
Lismore

St. Ita
Cappoquin

St. Ita
Loughrea

Brendan's Voyage

Brendan had often gone home to visit his foster mother. She suffered much during his first month away from her, but, as a good Christian, she had borne the loss stoically and with fortitude, for she believed that she had given Brendan to the service of God.

Now Brendan had grown to manhood. He was a princely figure. As Niall or Fergus or Erc had no more to teach him, his first call was to Ita. They sat together in the fort, he telling her about Jarlath who lived near to Tuam, Co. Galway. Ita said that Jarlath was the best scripture scholar in Ireland and they spoke also of the God to whom they both had dedicated their lives.

They spoke for a very long time, recalling the years when they had been together, but the time came for him to go once more. He began to walk towards the gate, but still he delayed.

"Mother, it will only take a few years before I will be ordained and I will become a Holy Man," he told her.

"I know that Brendan," she replied softly. "I taught you that the three things most pleasing to God are, a True Spirit with a True Faith and generosity. You and I who love to give, must remember that our motive should be one of Divine Charity. However little we give, it must be for the Love of Christ."

With that he prepared to go and she stood and watched him as he went from her into the distance.

*   *   *   *   *

Five years later, Brendan came home again and the people crowded around him. Women cried with sheer joy, for his kinspeople thought they had no hope of ever seeing him again. They clasped his hand and hugged him dearly. He told them of his travels far across the ocean, of the new lands he had seen and the adventures he and his fellow sailors had had on their long voyage.

He had not found his 'promised land', but, no matter, Brendan was home. Stories spread around Munster about the experiences he had had and what he had seen.

In time, Brendan came to visit Ita again.

"Brendan my love, why did you go on such a dangerous journey without telling me?" she asked. "You should have known that my heart would ache while you were gone, but all is well again, you are back."

That evening, Ita gathered together her young women and her foster children, for she wanted everyone to listen to Brendan's stories of his travels. Ita herself sat beside him as he told them about their hunger and their fears. The children on Ita's lap and those who stood around Brendan were open mouthed in awe, their eyes fixed on the face of this man who had travelled so far. They gazed on the face of their hero.

In their minds, they travelled with him from island to island. They could feel the cold winds the sailors had suffered and pictured the little boat made of animal hides rising on the waves and battling with the elements. Brendan continued his story.

"One year, we could not find land on which to say our Easter Mass, but after many days, we sighted a treeless island. There was no inlet to secure the currach, but we managed to clamber over the slippery rocks onto the smooth surface. There I said our Easter Mass and we gave thanks for our survival so far and asked our God for his guidance and protection in our task ahead. When we had concluded, I would have put out to sea straight away but the crew asked to cook a meal. They lit a fire, and . . ." Brendan paused to heighten the drama, while Ita tightened her hold on the child she had sitting on her lap.

" . . . suddenly, the island shuddered."

"It's the Devil," commented one old woman, "Old Nick himself," as she became immersed in the story and was almost overcome by the great wonder of it all.

"Glory and praise to God," said Ita, for once taken by surprise. The little child on her lap stared at Brendan and such was his concentration on the story that he was unable to react.

"It shuddered beneath our feet," went on Brendan, "and subsided and plunged into the sea, scarcely giving us time to board our currach again. We had been standing on the back of a sleeping whale," he finished with a smile.

They would have listened to his stories all night, but soon it was time to rest. Crossing the fort by starlight, all they could think of were Brendan's tales of his escapades on the sea and his search for the new land.

"I did not find my paradise," Brendan said sadly, when he and Ita were alone. "Why did I fail? I thought if I let the boat drift, God would guide me there."

Ita told him that God helps those who help themselves.

"Could you not have taken the oars into your hands and rowed instead of waiting for a miracle, Brendan," she asked? Then she told him a story about Kilbarrymeaden, when she was scarcely fifteen years of age and living in her home country. She said that Jesus came and told her to go to a little strand near Boatstrand, where there lived an old shipbuilder. This is now known as Tráigh Míde Óg. There, she was to learn all she could about boat building from him. He was a wise old man and she learned a great deal from him about the making of boats, the best timber and materials to use, how to assemble them and make them waterproof.

The wise old boatbuilder had many sayings. "Put your trust in God," he would say, "and you will always come home safe, my girl."

Ita looked straight at Brendan and told him that when he had started building boats first, he should have come to her for advice.

As she gently chided him, her voice rose like any Irish mother's would. 'What were you thinking of, sailing to the land of promise in dead animal hide. You should have known that no blood has ever been shed on its sacred shores. You still have a lot to learn, my good boy.'

Then she softened her voice. "I have here a design of a currach. I had it in my head ever since you first thought of going on those voyages. Never again build with anything but timber. Go to those shipbuilders, tell them to build you a proper wooden vessel and take the responsibility yourself to steer it by the stars that God set in the vast sky for that great purpose."

"So you think there should be a next time," Brendan asked.

"I think so Brendan," replied Ita, for she had great faith in the ability of her first foster son. She would let him go from her once more, as the Holy Mother Mary would.

In March the following year, Brendan stood with Ita outside her chapel as he explained the building of the all timber currach to her. It was just as she had planned. She drew her father's Holy Sword from its scabbard and told him the stories about it and what happened with her father, good man that he was. He had sacrificed his all for her, she told Brendan, and went on to relate the tales of how she had conquered the Druids with her Holy Sword.

"Now, Brendan, I am getting old" she said. "I have no more use for it. I am sure God would wish for me to pass it on. I give it to you as my first foster son. I am sure it will keep you safe and help you find your promised land. May your ship bring you safely to the land you seek."

Brendan took Ita's two hands saying "Goodbye my mother"

"Goodbye Brendan, my boy." said Ita, "may God bring you to your promised land."

For a little while she sat alone. She and Brendan had spoken for a long while that day and, as they sat together now, he showed her the drawings of the ship he had built. He showed her where her advice and her designs were used to build it.

"It is a great ship, Mother," said Brendan, "you'll have to come to Kerry to see it when I return." The ship was manned by sixty monks who would go with Brendan. Ita pictured it cutting through the waves, sailing towards the sunset and the promised land, beyond a sea no man had ever crossed and returned to tell the tale. She wondered if she had been right to urge him to go.

*   *   *   *   *

Years passed, years in which Ita often thought of her foster son, Brendan and prayed for him every day and every night. She beseeched God to keep him safe and to return him to her with his mission completed successfully.

Strengthened by his faith, guided by the stars which the Lord had provided and buoyed on his own and the prayers of Ita, in due time, Brendan came home. Word of his return sped from Aran where he made his landing to the mainland and from there spread like wildfire among the small communities who had heard of Brendan's long journey across the unknown.

Long before Brendan could reach her, Ita knew in her heart that his paradise had been found. Now, once more the Navigator strode through the gates towards her, carrying nothing but a leather bag, his white brat flowing behind him. His grey hair was bleached and tattered by the winds of the sea as he sailed towards a fame whose light would never fade.

Brendan stayed with his foster mother, recounting to her and the people of Kileedy, the full story of his discoveries. They listened in awe to his words and as he spoke they visualised with him the land of promise. He told Ita he did not bring back her holy sword and recounted to her how he came to part with it. Early one morning, a young King had come to him, mounted on a white horse. This king had been unsuccessful in his battles and, one night, he had a dream in which he saw Brendan leading his army. Brendan had explained he was not a fighting man and his only contest was for souls.

The king then asked for Brendan's sword, as he had also had a dream about the miraculous properties of the weapon which had come from Ita. Brendan told him to return in three days and he would give him his answer. He prayed all night, asking God for guidance. The king returned as he had been instructed and Brendan gave him the sword. The king assured Brendan he would do no wrong with Ita's sword.

"He returned again in two weeks," Brendan told Ita," "and thanked me gracefully and my God for the help he had received. He had won all his battles since receiving the holy sword and wanted to know all about the God whom we worship. It took a great deal of time to make him understand. Still he had faith in the sword and called it the Hand of God. We stood with him on silver sands and touched fruit that was autumn ripe. He told us about Judes who was marooned on a rock, to whom Satan and other spirits came and tried to take back to Hell. He asked me to give him some more time. Once every hundred years he got some time away from them before being taken back."

It was a fascinating story and his audience would have listened to him all night long. It was late, however, and Ita clapped her hands and said it was time for bed.

The next morning Brendan set out for Rosscarberry, Co. Cork to teach for a while in Fachtna's College.

Fachtna the Eloquent

Fachtna was born on the border of Waterford and Cork, somewhere near the river Blackwater. He was sent by his parents at an early age to Killeedy, Co. Limerick to the Holy Woman Ita. Even when he was very young, he spent much of his time studying the Sacred Scriptures. In later life, he went on to specialise in art, law and poetry and he also studied the conflict of religion in the early Roman Empire. He possessed a rare power, in that he was able to give vivid illustrations of his teachings. He was generous and steadfast and loved to address assembled crowds. His skill earned him the name, Fachtna the Eloquent.

His first school was set up near his homeland, beside Youghal and, after some time, Ita asked him to move to Rosscarberry. He soon became Abbot of the famous monastery there and students flocked from all parts of Ireland and Cornwall to study under his guidance. Learned men came from all over Ireland, some even arrived from Rome and the Far East to hear the famous orator speak. Shortly after returning from his famous voyage, Brendan came from Tralee to meet Fachtna as he wanted to share his knowledge with his students. Brendan remained teaching in Rosscarberry, discovering that his learned colleague was blind. Brendan implored him to let him inform their foster mother, Ita of his plight, but Fachtna would not relent. Brendan stayed teaching in the Monastery for two years and then left to build a monastery himself.

One evening, while Ita was out riding, she stopped to converse with a travelling monk. He told her the sad story of how the famous college of Rosscarberry would have to close down, as the great scholar and master had lost his sight and Brendan the Voyager had left for some unknown reason. Ita was taken aback by the news and hurried back to the Fort, giving orders to the men to get horses ready.

The next morning, Ita and eight men mounted their horses and rode through rough country, reaching Kilmeady, near Millstreet in Cork on the first night. There, she rested with her people and her holy men; those who looked after her church and who were now glad to see her. The next morning they continued on their journey through the countryside and, towards evening, they came to Killeedy, near Crossbarry. There, the saint visited the schools and her people who were delighted to see the Holy Woman in their midst. Their horses were taken care of and stabled for the night. Although tired, she talked to her people for two hours, then retired to rest in preparation for the last leg of the journey the following morning. The full journey of nearly ninety miles was not easy, travelling across rough terrain, often through woods and bushes.

On the final day, they found that the countryside was not as rough or as dangerous as was previously the case and the band of riders was able to make better time, arriving early in the afternoon in Rosscarberry. Although the great and eloquent man was totally blind, they found him out walking on the strand. His foster mother went to him and, putting her arms around him she said 'My son, my son' as tears filled her eyes.

"You could have sent for me when you needed me most," she gently chided him. Fachna knelt at the edge of the water and said: "I must have offended God in some way, or misguided my students in some fashion. I had to know I was forgiven before I could send for you."

Ita laid her hand on her foster son's head and prayed to the Most Holy Spirit to restore His humble servant's sight. She was casting out any evil spirits and was fighting for his soul as Satan and other evil spirits were crowding in, wanting to take for themselves this great soul. They prayed together for hours.

"Holy Spirit, come now in our hour of need, the Father, Son and Holy Ghost," they prayed. Soon the battle was won. The evil spirits moved out and clean spirits took their place.

Ita and her son thanked God and, as he rose to his feet, he discovered that his sight had been restored. Ita enquired if he could see as well as he could have previously.

"My dear mother," he exclaimed, "do you see those goats on the mountain?"

"I cannot see any goats at all," said Ita.

"I can distinguish from here, the male from the female," said Fachtna.

"Praised be to the Blessed Trinity," said the Virgin Ita, "God never closes one gap but he opens another."

Dying Abbot

Abbot Comhgán was old when he settled in the mountains near to Ita. She was glad to have him close by and, when needed, he often gave talks to her boys and sometimes took them to his monastery for a short stay. He always talked about the animals, the surrounding areas and how all of nature is related to God. He would also explain that all of nature, including themselves, was God. As people, they were images of God, he would say and he advised them to give themselves to the Lord. When God created us, he told them, He left a little hole in our hearts. We might have all the luxuries of this world, he would say, we might have worldly pleasures in abundance, but that when the joy of achieving them has passed and when the benefits themselves are gone, what then? We are left with the hole in our hearts. God is waiting for us and only the Lord alone can fill it. When it is filled, we have all the joy in the world and only then can we feel complete. Be good to Ita, your mother, he would advise, listen to the Holy Woman and be guided by her, for she will lead you to God.

The old Abbot was so ageless that his monks half expected he would continue to offer Mass and make the rounds of their cells until the Son of Man came in a cloud with the full power and majesty of Heaven. They wondered why God seemed to have forgotten his good and faithful servant. But the Lord had not forgotten him and now at last the year and the day which had been ordained for his homecoming had arrived and the old Abbot lay dying. One by one the monks filed into his cell. They could hardly believe that this could be the end of such a long and fruitful life and they knelt close to him, remaining there while he received Holy Viaticum, the food for his final journey.

As they knelt down in sadness beside him, the old Abbot kissed each of his sons farewell and turned to the Prior.

"Bring Ita to me before I die," he requested of him. The Prior who knew of the great friendship between the Abbot and Ita went to summon her at once. It was a grey June evening when the Abbot arrived at her monastery and the Abbess, Ita was preparing to receive the daughters of Ciarraigh Luachra, the Chieftain from Kerry. When he arrived, the Prior met her running out of her cell, with armfuls of sheepskin covering. She was making clothes for the poor.

"My Abbot is dying," he told her, "can you come to him. He wants you." She glanced around and asked Emer and Brighde to accompany her. Without waiting to say more, she and her companions were gone.

When they arrived, Ita spoke to the young women before entering the thatched cell where her friend lay dying,

"You will have the privilege," she told them, "of seeing how a saint dies." With that, she moved into the cell and, eager to see the dying Holy Man, the young women tiptoed in behind her.

A monk who sat close to the Abbot, rose to let Ita take his place. She looked into the face of her old friend and saw that his eyes were larger now than they normally were and looked watery. His face was twisted and his whole body seemed to be in pain. He fixed his eyes on her and, for a moment they cleared as if an intelligence behind them had reawakened.

- 119 -

"I'll soon die of this sickness," he said loudly and slowly, as if he was making every effort to be understood. "I'll soon die of this evil and I ask you in the name of Christ, at the hour in which I fall asleep, to lay your hands on my lips and close them. I know that if you do this for any dying man, the Angels of God will come themselves to lead that soul to Heaven."

His words shocked her. "What are you saying, my father," she asked him and, turning to the other monks asked: "What does he mean?"

"I don't know," whispered the Prior, "maybe he is beginning to wander. He can't last much longer with this pain." But the old man roused himself and again he commanded her: "Lay your hands on my lips, virgin. Let me feel the touch of your holy hands on my lips." She bent down to plead with him. "Father," she said, "it was to ask your blessing that I came and not to give you mine. Bless me and the young girls I have with me, before God takes you to Himself."

The Abbot still looked steadily at her, not just at her as a woman, but at the Spirit which was within her.

"Father, think of all you have done for God," she said gently, "think of the reward that is waiting for you in Heaven. You will be glorious, my father, with a high place among the saints. A sinner might ask my blessing, what need of it have you?"

She spoke quickly and anxiously, not thinking that the words she used could bring little comfort to a dying man.

"Your eyes can already half see God," she continued. "God's mercy, not ours makes the bridge from death to heaven."

But the man scarcely followed her, so gripped was he by the thought of his coming death and the fears it held for him. With the virgin at his side, he felt he had someone who would come between him and the evil spirits, he knew were crowding all around him in his cell. They were fighting for his soul, trying to push him towards hell. He wished that those around him would pray more urgently. He wished he could feel the virgin's hand.

"Do what I say," he pleaded and made a sign for Ita to obey. "Do what I ask this time," he said and his words were shrill. The evil spirits were determined to bring this old enemy of theirs to hell. He had fought them all his life, never yielding to their temptations. Satan now sent his strongest envoy to capture this offending soul, to punish him for all the young souls he had taken away from him. As a youth, the Abbot always pushed those evil spirits out. Now, it was Satan's hour. Now, it was payback time.

"Do what I ask and Satan will draw back," he pleaded and, suddenly those around him grew afraid. They could feel the evil spirits. They knew now what was going on. They knew that Abbot Comhgán could see them. The young Holy Women began to weep when they thought of what Ita had said, that they would see how a saint meets his death. Was this the ending God gave to a life lived only for him?

Ita spoke no more, but laid her fingers upon her friend's lips and waited. His eyes grew calm again. His breathing ceased. She felt his face warm to her touch and wondered if his soul had slipped through to Heaven or was it still struggling with the forces of darkness. She prayed for him to the Blessed Trinity, entreating, by the Blood of Christ, succour for her holy friend.

But the battle was already won, for now, other spirits filled the cell. It felt like a choir of angels had come and taken his soul through to Heaven. The young women began to hum together in a low voice. They had seen something wonderful after all.

Having seen the old man pass to his eternal reward, Ita and her two companions returned in silence to Cluain Credail. Ita had not been afraid of death in childhood and in girlhood she had seen her father's allies carried back to Kilmeaden from the battlefield dead, dying and injured. In later years she had attended to their wounded herself, so there was little new for her in death.

It was not the presence at his passing that saddened her but the loss of one who had been her confessor and good friend. The loss was all the greater for one who had a responsibility for souls as grave as hers. She did not know when Erc might return to the coast, for his journey was a long one. She had leaned on these friends and now, both of them had gone. Then in spite of her pain, she almost smiled for God had made it plain that she was to have no one but Him.

Bullrushes Child Like Moses

One day, one of Ita's Holy Women was walking by the riverbank. She heard a cry and peered into the darkness. Was it a lamb or a bird, she wondered? No, it must be a child's cry that she had heard. Still, there was no one on the rough road or in the brush or the clearing close by. But where did the noise come from? Then she noticed a basket. All manner of thoughts ran through her mind. She picked up the basket and saw there was a tiny baby inside. She thought of the story of 'Moses in the bullrushes' and, 'the child in the basket'.

"Oh, little lamb, oh, where did you come from at all," Ita murmured to herself. "You poor little garsún,"she purred over him. Then she ran with the baby to her Mother Abbess, smiling to herself to think of the surprise she would get.

"I am a lucky girl," she thought to herself 'won't Mother be pleased.'

"What have you brought me, dear child," the Abbess asked, with all the astonishment the young woman hoped for.

"A new foster son, Mother," Ita replied. "He was left outside the fort in a lovely basket. He looks like the baby of a queen, with such rich clothes he is wrapped in. It must be providence. We are so lucky, Mother. I am so excited."

"Hush child," said the Abbess, "and let me think." She thought she guessed the reason for the little child's abandonment, but would she ever know for sure? Who was she to question the Will of God?

In the days and weeks following, Ita kept the little boy beside her as much as she could. She and the other Holy Women would spend all their spare time thinking of names that they could call him. None was beautiful enough, or had the deep significance that this special child's name should have, so they continued to call him Cumméne, the child they found in a basket.

Then one day, as Ita sat outside in the warm sunshine with the child in her arms, she noticed that a woman was approaching alone,

Politely, the woman gave the information and sat down nearby. As she spoke with Ita and her friends, she kept her eyes on Cumméne.

"Is that Aedh, Lady Flann's child," she asked.

"I know nothing of his parentage," the Abbess replied. "I do not even know his name. We call him Cumméne because we found him in a basket."

"This is Flann's son," said the strange woman, "it is on his account, my lady, that I am here." She paused for a short while, before resuming her questioning.

"So you know nothing of him then," she asked? "Nothing whatever of the circumstances of his birth?"

"Nothing," replied the Abbess, now on her guard, "but I can guess that you are going to tell me."

"His parents were unmarried," replied the woman.

"Then tell me at once what you know about this child," said the Abbess with authority, "I must know his name and the circumstances of his arrival here."

As the woman began her story, a sense of revulsion stole over Ita. She had to close her eyes from the now sinister beauty of the child in her arms.

"Prince Fiachra was visiting the Chieftain of Lough Léin," began the woman, hesitantly. "When the chieftain asked his daughter Flann to show their visitor the sights of their mountain and lakes, the beautiful girl of sixteen agreed. They set off on horseback, near the close of a fine summer's day. Shortly after, they got caught in a heavy shower on the mountainside and entered a cave to shelter from the shower. After sweet talking Flann with his charm, he took advantage of the young girl and, later that evening, after a good meal in the hospitality of the Chieftain, he mounted his fine horse and rode away, never to come back again. Later, it emerged that Flann was to have his child and she was in a sorry state as she was betrothed to another man. She never told anybody, even her mother. She begged me to help her, making me swear on the Holy Book to keep her secret."

The woman went onto explain that in the final weeks before she was to have the child, she asked the girl's father to let her take his daughter away to the mountain, explaining that it was for her health's sake. The Chief had an abode out on the mountain, so he agreed.

"I know I was taking a great risk," continued the woman, "but I felt I had to do something for her. I tell you, Lady, it was a long, long month out there and lonely too, but we survived. One morning, at the break of day, a son was born to her and everything turned out right. I believe that it was the will of God which directed her to send him here, for you would know how to manage such things. That is how she sent him here. She thinks we gave the child, in return for a few cows, to some poor childless couple who would gladly rear him."

As the woman looked at the child, Ita tightened her hold on him, a fierce and protective love flowering in her heart.

"You will never make me part with him," she told the woman, looking straight into her eyes.

"But such a child will bring a curse on you and on your household," replied the woman in astonishment. "It was only for your good that I told you all this, anxious as I was to protect a virgin of Christ, whom all Munster venerates. Can you not see that you must send away this infant, who can bring nothing but evil, seeing that he himself is the fruit of an evil deed?"

"Dear woman," Ita replied, and her strange words were prophetic of the childís preordained sanctity. "Do not call this child cursed, for the creation of a child is a Divine deed, full of grace."

It was a few moments before the woman replied.

"Then Lady, I will leave him to you and to God, since He so urges you to keep him," said the woman.

"When you return," said Ita, 'tell Flann that I have made him my own son.'

"I will tell her that," said the now joyful woman, "I will explain to poor Flann, little more than a child herself when she gave birth, that she is hardly to blame for the tragedy"

The words ascribed to St. Ita are: 'Nach olc an gníobh é. Uair as gniomh déanta, de gráth mar é. Do you think she would like to come and live with us here?î

"No," replied the woman, "The Eoghanach of Loch Léin are a powerful and important family and have already arranged an important match for Flann. God grant she will be happy."

"God grant she may be," said Ita, as she looked into Cumméne's eyes. "You are the son of a prince," she told him sadly, "the lord of Loch Léin, Woods and hills."

Cumméne, who did not understand, only drummed his heels until he made his foster mother smile. After a hearty meal, the woman set out on her return journey to Loch Léin. All the holy women were pleased. Cumméne had really come home, where love for him was unbounded and his mother lived as a Holy Woman during the later years of her life.

Cumméne of Clonfert, grandson of Fiachra, King of West Leinster, studied at Saint Finbarr's school in Cork and later became renowned as the learned and ascetic bishop of Clonfert. At the same period, his half brother, King Guaire ruled over that region.

After a life of great sanctity and service to God, Cumméne died in 621. He is revered as a saint and his Feast Day is 12th November.

Abbot of Clare

Early one morning, a messenger came to Ita from her foster son Brendan, asking for a favour. A young friend named Luchtigherna was dying from a wound he had received in a skirmish with thieves while they were stealing cattle from him. This was a common occurrence at that time, as the population was mostly unruly and warlike. This was the time when Brendan was about to leave on his first voyage and he asked Ita to cross the Shannon by boat to tend to the wounded Luchtigherna. She went on to Ennistymon in the present County Clare, where she healed Brendan's friend, as well as several other people who were also sick. There were many disputes she had to settle, advice she had to give to her people and things she had to teach them.

She had no trouble from the local Druids as they were afraid to confront her. They knew she was coming and knew also of her reputation as a fighter and as a Holy Woman. They knew of her

Ennistymon Site of Ita Church

powerful God and her holy sword and, most of all, they knew of her battles in Munster.

She stayed just four months in Ennistymon and, in that time, she had many converts. She built a school and found people to teach there. She was known to instill knowledge quickly into people in order that they should become teachers themselves. She also built a church with the help of Luchtigherna, the youth whom she had healed. He became known as Abbot of Clare and soon, he also became one of her dearest friends.

Brendan Rescues Wronged Maiden

Ita lived among the people of Hy Connail for a long time and came and went as necessary on her many missions. She met and dealt with all manner of difficulty, trials and troubles and obeyed God's every command. She had to prove that His mercy was great. Her mind went back over her years in her vocation. She remembered war, death, sickness and loneliness and Ita believed that she had been spared no pain by Christ. How wrong she had been in this belief, for she did not realize how little she knew about Divine ingenuity and how God devises means of perfecting the souls of those worthy people whom he loves.

One day, the members of her community were gathered together waiting for their Holy Mother on earth to come to them as she always did, to tell them of the gospels, or to converse with them on what they had learned in prayer. Sometimes they seemed to talk about nothing, sometimes they sang the songs she composed. It was part of their lives. But this day she delayed in coming and when at last she did arrive, her Holy Women saw that she had been weeping. They looked away, troubled by what they had seen. None of them had ever before seen her break down. They had taken her strength and fortitude so much for granted, for they thought her a saint of God. She herself thought that nothing could hurt her, but now, with her tears, her humanity was all too plainly revealed.

Ita tried to speak to her Holy Women. She had prepared many words for them but she could use none of them. She looked from one face to another and when they looked at her, they saw that her face had aged and it was colourless. Then with an effort at self control, she spoke to them.

"This day one of our household has sinned . . ." But she could not continue. She stood up and returned to her cell. The Holy Women looked at one another, amazed at what they had heard. What had she meant, they asked among themselves? They had not seen or heard anything that day or any other day which should cause her such distress. Ita had not explained her words.

In silence, they followed her from the room, each one feeling that she could not go back to her tasks, whether in the sacristy, the outhouse dairy, or the vegetable plot, until she knew for certain that it was not she who had sinned. They knew the Abbess was a reader of souls. What had she seen? An unworthy sinner! Each woman searched her own soul. Each feared she might be the guilty one and so first one and then another went to the Abbess and throughout the day continued to seek her, until each one had received from her the assurance that she was innocent.

Then a lonely figure of a girl called Segnith came to Ita. It was for her that Ita had waited and she now stood up and held out her arms to the girl. She spoke in a low voice to Segnith asking "Why did you trouble so little to preserve the virginity that you promised to Christ?" Angrily denying the charge, the girl left her and left the fort that night, all the while crying bitterly.

Ita wept and felt she had let herself down. Somehow she knew she had not done the right thing. God had put her to the test and she had failed. The ugly rumors flew around and it was said a woman like that should not be in charge of young people.

"It is not much good being a wonder worker, if you can't even govern your own monastery," said the gossips. The scandal was spreading. An old widow said; "You call that woman a prophetess? Did she not know that that fellow was coming in and out of the Monastery any time he pleased. She should be driven from our countryside. We must have better women here in Hy Connail."

St. Ita's Shrine at Kileedy, Co. Limerick

Although Princess Ita was poor at heart and felt sad, she still looked after the needs of the people. When the winds turned bitter in the early spring, all the old gossips headed for the shelter and hospitality which Ita

St. Ita's Well Kileedy,
Co. Limerick.

offered in Killeedy. Before long the scandal that had once threatened to destroy her was forgotten. In time, even the young Holy Women forgot it. It drew them closer to their Abbess because of the disgrace they had so lately shared.

But Ita herself could not forget it. Sometimes she knelt at the back of the chapel, watching as others prayed. Before the Blessed Sacrament, she would think of the words of Jesus 'Of those You have given to Me, I have not lost any'. Christ had given her that child to foster, made her guardian of His bride's virginity. Why had she been so preoccupied with other things, that she could not see that the girl needed sympathy and guidance. She wondered if they had driven her to Hell.

Segnith, she knew, had left the Rath unrepentant, in the pangs of childbirth. She may have died. Ita could still see in her mind the hurt and mistrust in the young face.

"I surely have failed You and my daughter, oh Jesus," she accused herself. She hid her face in her hands as she prayed for her daughter's soul, as she rested in prayer with God.

As time passed, Ita would not allow the memory of Segnith or her plight to go from her mind. Then one night Jesus came to her in a dream, accompanied by His Blessed Mother. Mary told her she was still taking care of the young girl and her child and Jesus told her that despite what had happened, Segnith was doing His work well.

Then the explanation which Ita had so wished for came. The Druids and their evil ones had conceived a plan to blacken Ita and have her driven out. They were afraid of her God and her holy sword and what they could not do by force they decided to achieve by stealth.

They devised a plan to blacken Ita, divide her community and eventually get rid of her. Five of them set upon Segnith and with no thought for the girl, raped her. The girl was utterly ashamed of what happened and believed nobody could understand what happened to her. She did not know who her attackers were. One thing she did know was that they were evil men and that as a result of their actions, she was expecting a child.

In her despair, she could not see mercy anywhere, not even from Ita herself. She felt as if evil spirits had taken her over, so she went out into the dark night and adding loneliness to her shame, she roamed the countryside. Eventually, the Druids took her in and made her their slave. When her little girl was born, they claimed her as their own and there she stayed for several years. Segnith had to work hard and often wondered, amid her beatings, humiliations and suffering, what would become of her child. Many times she whispered a prayer to the Virgin Mary, but, in her innocence and guilt, she thought she was not worthy of being answered.

Now that she knew the truth, Ita sent word to Brendan, explaining the whole story. As it was not far from Tralee, she asked him to go to the Druids' grove and rescue Segnith. Brendan went to the Druids' Fort, arriving as they were about to make a sacrifice to Baal. Some were gaunt with white robes, their ears straining for secrets hidden in the stars. One had a raven sitting on his shoulder, croaking loudly. They all stopped what they were doing when the tall, athletic form of Brendan entered. He demanded the release of the woman they had so falsely taken and enslaved. They denied all charges and refused to release her and her daughter. Brendan warned them he would return again with dire consequences for them.

As good as his word, Brendan returned to the Druids Grove with seventeen men. This time he was wielding Ita's holy sword. He told the Druids that their whole clan would be wiped out if they did not release the mother and child. They would also have to confess to the horrific crime they had committed. The Druids gathered together in a circle for a few moments. They shook and trembled at the sight of the sword and, wisely, they agreed to give the woman and her child into the care of Brendan.

They had read in the stars that their way of life was coming to an end and that Christianity was going to take over from them.

They also made a full confession of how, when and where they had committed the crime. What was more amazing, they asked Brendan if he would instruct them in the religion he practiced, that they too might become Christians. This he did gladly and, after several visits, they became Christians.

Segnith and her child returned to Killeedy to Ita's open and welcoming arms. Segnith could doubt no longer. She acknowledged the mercy of God was greater than any sin. She had also witnessed the power of God as one after another, the Druids fortresses had fallen. Each Holy Woman put her hands around her and cried on her shoulder, begging her forgiveness. She then went to Ita and cried in her arms, happy at last.

Ita's Evil Uncle Freed from Purgatory

Fifty years after her encounter with her suitor, Loe Ghuire, Ita had visions of events in the other world. Her evil uncle from Coolfin, who lived in Kilmeaden on the banks of the Suir and who had wished for her to marry Loe Ghuire for his own selfish ends, had been killed during his misadventure in trying to kidnap Ita for the Druids. Ita, through her visions, saw him suffering in purgatory and she sent for his four sons and told them that the manner of his sufferings had been revealed to her. To help him, she said, each one of them must give alms to the poor every day for the whole year, for the benefit of his soul and then at the end of the year return to her. They were wealthy people and did as she asked. At the end of the year they came back to Ita and she told them that their alms-giving and prayers had helped their father, but they must continue their donations for another year.

At the end of that second year, on their return to Ita, she told them that for the following year they had to clothe the poor as their father had not done so in the name of Christ and for this he was still suffering. Having obeyed her orders they met again with Ita at the end of that third year. She informed them that due to their constant prayers and alms-giving their father was now enjoying eternal rest.

Faithlegge
Boohan, Skilful Warrior and Craftsman

The King of New Ross was at war with several chieftains from his neighbouring Wexford who had joined forces to beat him. He had five sons who were intensely loyal to him under any circumstances. They were fighting in five different places, with a hundred men with each prince. Boohan was one of the sons defending their homeland. He got word that his father was wounded and that his life was in danger and needed Boohanís help. Boohan withdrew from the fight with eight of his men, leaving the rest to fight on. He arrived to his father just in time and he and his men fought hard and furiously. They managed to get the king on a horse, taking him out of danger.

Now, only seven men were left fighting their fifteen opponents and were beginning to tire. It was only a matter of time until those who outnumbered them would see them killed. Then a group of reinforcements came to their rescue and their foes quickly scattered. Although still standing, those gallant fighters were badly wounded and if they did not get medical aid they would soon die. It was decided to take them to Faithlegge in Waterford to a safe house. They moved in two boats, twenty two men in each boat and entered the Suir somewhere near Dunganstown. They rowed hard and arrived in Faithlegg in two hours, just as it was getting dark. One of

The landing spot at Faithlegge as it still is today

their comrades died before they managed to reach the landing site, a place that is still in existence to this day.

By chance, Ita's sister Nessa happened to be visiting her uncle at the moate where the warriors were taken. Although a very young

The modern surround of the old well at Faithlegge

The Moate at Faithlegge

girl, she volunteered to nurse them. She knew enough that unless she had Divine help, they would not live too long, especially Boohan, their leader.

Nessa had had an unusual experience as she had gone to fetch water from the nearby well. She saw what she thought was the reflection of the Child Jesus in the well. She was startled for a moment and looked again. She saw another boy offering gifts to the

The Old Church at Faithlegge, site of St. Ita's Church.

"Faithlegg Castle (Aylward's Castle) in 1840 by Charles Newport Bolton. The castle was abandoned in the 1770s and rapidly became ruinous. Virtually nothing now remains. This sketch, which was all that remained of the Castle up to 1956. It collapsed that year and is now almost non-existant."

Divine Child and vaguely recognized the second child as someone of her own family or friends. Still it puzzled her. She looked a second time and all that was to be seen was two little golden fishes.

Now, with seriously wounded men to nurse, she needed help. She went into a quiet room and communicated with her sister, Ita. She knew Ita was praying so she went on her knees for two hours, holding a picture in her hand of the Divine Child which Ita had sent her. She promised the Lord that if He spared the young man, his companions would do something positive to win souls for God. She knew in her heart that they would fulfil her promise.

In two days, the six youths were almost better and sitting up without a care or a worry. They wanted to know all about Ita, as they knew someone or something had a hand in their getting better. When they were sufficiently improved, they willingly built a church and a school for Ita and her Living God. The well, which is a very attractive one, is still known as St. Ita's well and is beautifully decorated and still venerated today.

*   *   *   *   *

The lives of the wild young warriors who had been saved were changed completely. They became kind and helpful youths and they could not do enough for Nessa and the people of Faithlegg. Everybody loved the young men. They brought life into the community and showed great gratitude for what had been done for them. However, it was time for the young warriors to move on. As they were skilled fighting men, they were given the offer of joining the forces of Conla, Kennfoelad's right hand man and one of the most distinguished noblemen of the Decies. He had survived the battle of Gortroe to lead the Kilmeaden men in more battles.

As it was difficult to find good and loyal fighters at that time of severe conflict, Boohan became leader of the Kilmeaden men and protected the fort even when his own life was in danger. He served for five years and was then given his own land and became a free man, a nobleman in his own right again, in a different part of the country. He built a stone house for himself on his land. Not only had he a reputation as a warrior, he had an honoured profession as a skilled stone mason. At that time, stone-building was looked on as a very practical skill. His house was viewed with envy by many chieftains, near and far. Even Ita wanted him to build churches and schools for her. But he found himself praying constantly, as he now had become a Christian.

As Boohan prayed, a door opened in his mind. He saw a line that led directly to God. Up until now, his status was not great in life. Now he stood as he had done in his own country a proud and free man. He could now ask for any woman's hand. He could recall Nessa as she nursed him and his wounded comrades in Faithlegge in the Waterford estuary. She was a mere child then. Now he knew why he came to Kilmeaden by the banks of the river Suir. Nessa lived in her father's fort. She had grown into a beautiful and mature woman. He had often watched her run across the fort, sometimes in her bare feet and had laid a hand on his heart and prayed she might return his love.

He thought of the infants she had seen in the well. Now he was decided, so he dressed in his best Celtic clothes, went to her parents and asked for her hand in marriage. He told them he could give the dowry, the marriage gift which noblemen gave to parents. He was to be disappointed though, for when Nessa was asked, she did not consent to be his wife. She thanked him saying that she had thought about going to her sister to give her life to God. She told him to come back in four weeks, when she would give her answer.

For days she prayed, asking Jesus for guidance. Then she communicated with her sister Ita and she told her she had a free will to do whatever she wanted. God had different ways for people to do His Divine will, Ita told her and that night she had a dream. She saw Jesus talking to a little child. She recognized the child for he was one of her own, as she had seen in the well in Faithlegg. The Lord was watching over him.

Again it was Bealtaine. Boohan dressed, putting on his 'brat' and his sword. He was ready once more to meet Nessa. He mounted his steel grey horse and rode towards Rath. He looked like a warrior on his way to battle. On his arrival, a boy took his horse and he moved forward with hope in his heart, that he might succeed on his great personal mission on this occasion.

He loved Nessa as much as life itself and it had been a long four weeks. He had worked hard, so hard that he had a building completed. It was difficult asking for Nessa's hand a second time and he wondered what he would do if she said no. It was now in God's hands, he told himself and moved to meet Conla.

Conla bade him welcome, then he and his wife left Boohan and Nessa alone. Nessa told him she had given the future much thought and that she wished to spend it with Boohan. He was overjoyed and delighted that their hour had come at last. From then on they both lived as one.

They had a quiet wedding, said goodbye to family and friends, mounted their horses and rode into the sunset to their home. In the following year, Boohan constructed many fine buildings and then, after twelve months, a son was born to them. There was great rejoicing in the Rath, in the area now known as Kilmagemoge.

Their first-born was a divine child from the day he arrived. He was christened Mo-choem-og, my fair youth. He lived a happy life in the fort, now called Magemogue, in the modern Kilmeaden. When he was twelve years of age, he was sent on horseback to his aunt, the Holy Woman, Ita, in Killeedy in Limerick. He was to become a Holy Man.

Thurles, Co. Tipperary

Ita's nephew and foster son, established a church in Liath Mór or Leagh Mor, near Thurles in Co.Tipperary. He was afterwards known as Saint Mochoemog, the Latin version of which is St. Pulcherius whose Feast Day is on the 20th May. Mochoemog was young and enthusiastic and he embraced everything about God. He brought the word of Jesus to its people and made them Christians.

Drawing of Mochoemog's Large Church near Thurles

When Mochoemog was leaving his Aunt's College at an early age, he asked the Holy Woman Ita where he should set up his first Church. She handed him a little dumb bell saying he should travel for two nights and two days until he heard the bell sounding. Mochoemog set out and when he heard the bell sounding he was

Ancient Drawing of Leigh Oratory

overjoyed and gave thanks to God, for he knew he was in the right place.

There he found a great wild hog whose colour was liath or grey and so he decided that the place should henceforth be called Liath Mor. In honour of the Holy Man, it later became Liath Mochoemog, where the Principal Church of St. Mochoemog was established. This was at the place presently known as Two Mile Borris in Co. Tipperary, about four miles from Thurles and just a short distance removed from the old coach road between Cashel and Dublin. Those ruins and traces of the old ecclesiastical buildings may still be seen at Liath Mochoemog. Several disciples hastened to the place under his guidance. The people of the area loved him, thought him a sensation and flocked to hear his sermons.

Soon, Mochoemog wished to spread his wings and to build a church near Ardfinnan. An ancient road of St. Patrick ran close by, but the countryside was wild and rough. When the young Mochoemog decided to build a church, he had to leave in a hurry. There was a strong force of men in a nearby Rath and an even stronger force of Druids. They got on well enough together, but the Gaels would not offend them. It seemed that the Gaels

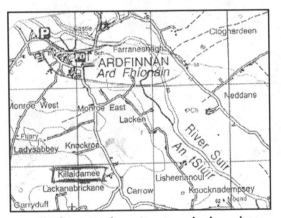

Killaidamee, where Ita stayed when she passed through Ardfinnan.

were under the influence of the Druids and they would not let Mochoemog build a church. He thought long and hard about what he should do. He thought it best to send a courier to his aunt Ita, informing her of the situation. The saint answered the call immediately and set out to go to Ardfinnan with five of her best swordsmen.

They came via St. Patrick's Road, but near what is now Clonmel, some robbers from the area, fifteen men in all, saw a woman on a white horse with five harmless looking men. Even better, they said among themselves, they were strangers. They would soon relieve the unwary travellers of their belongings. These men were ruthless and feared nobody. Some months before, they had ambushed the High Priest Druid and his men, leaving some of them wounded and his only son dying. The Druid or his gods could not help his son and he pledged that if he could catch the robbers, he would punish them.

Now, they viewed the strangers as easy prey, but only too soon though, they found out to their cost that Ita on her white horse could twist and turn in a split second and any of her men could equal five of the robbers. After several of the robbers were wounded, the ambushers soon found out that their fight was hopeless and begged for mercy. To their amazement, Ita spared them further casualties and healed the wounds of the fallen. They were very grateful, asked her for forgiveness and promised to give up their evil ways. They then mounted their horses and rode into the night.

As it was now getting dark, Ita went to the nearest fort. She was well known all over Munster through her great sword and her amazing power. The news of the fight with the robbers spread quickly and Ita was made welcome at the fort. The people were in mourning, for the Chieftain's sixteen year old daughter was dying. She had been poisoned by eating wild mushrooms, something which was not unusual at the time and now lay in a coma. Every local healer and every known remedy was tried and even the Druid priest was called. He tried everything and vainly called on his gods to make her well.

As soon as Ita came, the dying girl's mother went to her and explained what had happened to her daughter. After an hour's rest, Ita went to the room where the sick girl lay. She held her hand, closed her eyes, then spoke in a loud voice.

"Depart ye evil spirits, the Lord God of Hosts has come to this room. I speak in the name of Jesus, depart. Depart in the name of the

Blessed Trinity." Then a very loud and horrible noise was heard. A great fire burned in the big fireplace of the bedroom. Suddenly, the fire left the grate and went up the chimney. Then the room was peaceful and silent and the girl cried as if in pain. Ita spoke to her kindly.

"Come child, your mother is waiting for you," she said softly. The girl jumped up and flung herself into the Holy Woman's arms and clung to her. There was great rejoicing in the fort and the celebrations went on for several days. Even Ita showed she was human by joining in the happy event

The next morning, there was a loud knocking at the gate of the fort. It was the high priest from the Druid's grove, with ten of his men.

"I demand to see the great woman," he shouted. He was allowed in but his men had to stay outside. He came before the virgin and went down on his knees crying, hardly able to speak. "My son, my only son is dying," he sobbed. "Come, come with me graceful lady, I beg of you, come. I will not worship false gods any longer. Come and heal him for he is a good and obedient son to me."

The virgin left the fort with her men. The Druid and his men mounted and rode to their grove, entered and rode up to the big stone altar. There was a great flat stone on top, where the Druid's son lay, his body covered in the blood of a young calf. The calf's life had been offered to their gods in place of the young man's, but it was unsuccessful. The young man showed no sign of life at all. His colour was a deathly pale and his father said he was afraid they were too late.

"No," said Ita, confidently. "God has the final say in all things, have faith." She asked everyone to leave the grove except the Druid high priest. They knelt down on the lower slabs, three feet apart. She asked him to remove some of the young Druid's clothes.

"Now we must promise God that you will forsake all false gods,"she said, "never again to spill the blood of animals as sacrifices. Renounce Satan for we must give honour and praise to Our Lord Jesus Christ only. You must devote the rest of your life to Him. We will ask God to restore the life of your son."

Then she started to pray aloud.

"O Holy and Almighty God, we humbly ask you, that if it be your will, to come and give life to this young man, that he may live the rest of his life to serve and obey Your commandments."

The young man sat up, opened his eyes and spoke. There was great joy in his father's eyes and he shouted 'Praise be to the Living God. Forever I shall praise His name'. He called all his men, all his family and all the Druid priests together to announce the joyful news to them.

"God has given me back my son," he said, "henceforth, you all shall obey this God's commandments, the laws of the One, True and Living God whom we now serve. You shall listen to what the holy virgin says."

With all of the Gaels in the Rath turning to Jesus and the Druids becoming Christians, in one month they had a church and a school built. They became a very united people, a great Christian flock. The high priest Druid became Christian and a Holy Man, well able to perform holy rites. Many of the Druids became Christians and became close friends with the Gaels.

*   *   *   *   *

Ita returned to Killeedy to find that Mochoemog was pleased with the church and school. Now at last he was getting somewhere. The young Druid was scarcely nineteen and he and the chieftain's lovely daughter became close friends. Mochoemog turned his eyes towards Nenagh, but he could not establish a church there, for he would not be listened to, let alone be heard. It was a densely populated area which contained six rival clans, forever fighting against each other. The only service the youth was allowed to perform was to attend to their wounds. He was often invited to side with one clan or the other, but he knew it was not a thing a young Holy Man should do.

Then a fight broke out between two of the strongest Clans which lasted for several days. Many of the young men received serious wounds in the fighting, one of them a warrior who was betrothed to the chieftainís daughter. He was to become leader of the Clan when the chieftain became too old for fighting. Now, as he lay wounded, he was close to death and would surely die if he did not receive help quickly. They sent for Mochoemog and were excited and relieved when he came. He was asked many questions about his foster mother. "Where did she come from," they asked. "With whom had she fought? Why had she done such things?"

He was very careful in what he said. He told them she worked for Jesus, who could be an angry God if He was not obeyed. He would bring disaster upon people who were continuously fighting and killing and wounding each other. God wanted them to be peaceful, that they should love one another as He loved them. They asked Mochoemog if Ita would come and heal the wounded. The young Holy Man sent for his Aunt, Ita, asking if she would come to Nenagh to help the people there.

ST ITA
WINDOW,
NENAGH

Ita responded straight away and came on horseback with her five protectors. A large crowd of people gathered around the fort to catch a glimpse of her. She was told that if she healed the wounded, she could ask for whatever she wished. It took her two days to make her way through the six clans healing all the young fighting men.

In return, she asked for what she usually asked for, that a church be built in honour of the One, True God whom she served. The chieftain was only too glad to give his men to build a large church, thirty feet long and twenty-five feet wide, together with a school. Now Mochoemog had a church and school where he could teach the children and the young men and the young women to become good Christians and obey the word of God.

Clonmel

Some years after the fifteen robbers attacked Ita and she healed the wounded, one of their sons became a Holy Man. He came to Mochoemog asking for his help and said his people had given up their sinful ways and wished to build a church in honour of the virgin Ita and her Living God. Mochoemog immediately gave his approval. He was

Franciscan Friary, Clonmel, site of the first Church in the Clonmel area.

Statue of St. Ita in SS. Peter & Paul Clonmel

delighted, for it was not what he expected from them. He explained to them what was needed. The robbers gave a great deal of their time to building the church, now that they had given up their evil ways. In six months they had it finished and Ita was invited to come. She had many duties to perform in many locations however and was unable to be present for the great occasion.

This church was dedicated to Ita and Mochoemog, at its opening, spoke kindly of her with warmth and affection.

The Dawn River at Kilmagemogue

Moate at Kilmagemogue

which was strange in this part of the country. Ita greeted her, asked her name and where she had come from.

"She has done so much for our people," he said. "She has brought peace to all our people. She has brought the gift of God to us all. We honour her with all our hearts. We hope and pray that she will come to Clonmel again, if she can spare the time. She is forever doing the work of God and long may our great mother live."

Five years later, Ita visited Clonmel, saw her beautiful church and, as she was used to the unusual ways of God, was not surprised that it had been built by the robbers.

Kilmagemogue

Mochoemog received a message from his mother's people in Kilmeaden. It came from the great nobleman of the Decies, Conla, the head man who had served Ita's father King Kennfoelad. He had survived the battle in Clashmore where Ita's father had died along with his brother. Her uncle had died in Gortroe and all had lost their lives defending the Princess from her suitor, Prince Loe Ghuire, who wished to possess her at any price. After the battle, Conla returned safely to Kilmeaden and now he was Chief of the fort. Through his messenger, Conla told of a little girl who had been kicked in the head by his nephew's horse and was now in danger of death.

"Come, we are your people," he pleaded. "We would very much like to see you, so that you might help us in our time of need".

Mochoemog ordered two horses to be got ready for him and a friend. After two days ride, they arrived in Kilmeaden to a great welcome late in the evening. As soon as they had supper, he was taken to the nursery, where the little girl lay. He prayed over her and entreated the Lord to intervene on her behalf.

"I wish my foster mother was here with me now," he thought and he felt a sensation come over him. He sat on the bed and took the little girl in his arms, stroking her forehead. She sat up and opened her eyes and everyone was amazed. They said it was a miracle.

Mochoemog thanked God and Ita for their help and intervention that night. The people implored him to establish a church in Kilmeaden. He consented and it took three months to build. It was known as Kilmochoemog, now known as Kilmagemogue, the place of his birth.

Raised from the Dead

With time, Ita's sympathy towards suffering had strengthened. Years of contact with the heart of Christ had given her own heart a patience it had not always possessed and so she would listen to the long and sometimes tiresome stories of the lonely, or put out her hand to the sick as often as they came.

Late one evening, while the holy women were at prayer, a loud noise and sudden keening was heard outside the fort. Frightened by the eerie sobs, the choir dropped their voices, until only one woman continued singing the psalm.. Then another voice joined hers and a third and the chant continued, while the Abbess and a companion left to go to the entrance of Lios.

Ita's companion opened the gate a little and thrust her head out, half fearing to see the fairy hosts of Munster outside, making dirge for dead heroes. Instead, she saw no one but a peasant man. The Abbess opened the gates wider and went out to the man. He cried out again when he saw her and showed her the dead boy whom he held in his arms and whom he had carried many miles. His faith was rare.

"Do not cry, a mhic," said the Abbess "only tell me how I can help you."

"Cry I will," he replied roughly, "I'll stand here waiting until you bring my son back to life. And know for certain, Saint of God, I'll not leave this house until my prayer is heard."

The words were shouted angrily, for sorrow had half robbed the man of reason. Everyone looked at Ita, wondering what reply she would make. She paused and then answered him gently.

"It is only an apostle of Christ who could perform the miracle, such as you ask of me. As for myself, I am powerless, so let us pray instead that God may have mercy on this poor boy's soul."

"That's what I am grieving over," said the man. "He died without making his confession and without saying any word to me." He looked down at his son's pale face. The Abbess felt a great pity steal over her heart, but dare she ask God for such a favour? She looked at the father again.

"Ask the Holy Trinity to let my son live," he entreated "if only for one day so that I can hear his voice again before he goes from me altogether."

"God is merciful and thoughtful," said Ita. "He raised the dead to life when he walked among us as man. Suppose He were to have pity on you and restore your son to life, how long would you be content to have with him?"

"I would be grateful to have but one day," replied the poor man, "and then I would let him go to God."

Ita touched the boy's face. "You ask for only one day," she said, "but God is giving you fifteen years. After that time, when he is coming near his manhood, you shall bring him back here. We will train him to serve God."

The boy was restored to life and his father was overjoyed. As tears rolled down his face, he went home with his son and he lived a happy childhood.

Malahide - Mullach Íde

Finnan was born in Waterville, Co. Kerry about the 5th century, the son of noble parents. He developed an illness commonly called leprosy and was cured with herbs and ass's milk by an elderly Holy Woman from Kenmare. His mother said she would rather see him die than grow up to commit mortal sin. He did not grow up to be tall and the leprosy left him with a slight limp. Still, he was alert in

mind and was not inhibited in any way. His young companions said of him that he could fight like a tiger and swim like a fish.

At the age of twelve his parents sent him to his uncle, St. Brendan, to study to be a holy man. After two years of intense

Malahide Strand where Finnan landed.

preparation, and shortly before going on his voyage, Brendan sent him to Ita to finish his studies. Through her example and regular instruction, Finnan grew up to be valiant and loyal in every way.

In later years, as Ita grew older, Finnan was with her in all her missions. As time went on, she sent him out more and more to do her missionary work for her. He went out to make peace among the warrior tribes and was sometimes called upon to fight on one side or the other. He always said a fight was good if it fitted God's will and brought peace to the people. He became known as Candid the Peacemaker. He was loved, yet feared throughout Munster. He was a good ambassador for Ita and Jesus and, as she became confident in him, she found she could send him with confidence to any part of the country. On one particular occasion, she sent him back to Kilmeaden and Kilmagemoge to meet with Boohan and her sister Nessa with confidential messages, a long and dangerous journey.

*   *   *   *   *

Columba was born at Gartan in Donegal on 7th December 521. He was of the princely race of the Ui Néill, with ancestors going back to the Kings of Tara. He was baptized at Tulach-Dubhglaise, now Temple-Douglas, by a priest named Cruithneachan, who afterwards became his tutor or foster-father. His marked devotion to the Church, won him the name Colmcille (Dove of the Church).

Columba loved books and spared no pains to obtain them. Amongst the many precious manuscripts his former master had obtained in Rome, was the first copy of St. Jerome's Psalter to reach Ireland. Columba borrowed the book and surreptitiously made a copy for his own use. However when its owner, on being told what he had done, laid claim to the transcript, Columba refused to give it up. The matter was taken up before the law and the judgement which was given was a wise one and a precept which many remember to this day.

"To every cow, its calf," said the judge, "and to every book, it's copy. Therefore you must hand back the copy to the owner of the book." Columba resented the judgement. but he was soon to have much more serious grievances against King Diarmuid.

In a sporting contest between Connaught and Leinster, a player named Curran, on the Connaught side, after fatally injuring a player on the Leinster team, was set upon by his opponents. He managed to escape and took refuge with Columba. However, in defiance of the right of sanctuary in a holy place, he was dragged from his protectors and brutally slain by Diarmuid's men. Columba sided with the men from Connaught because of the lawless manner in which the Leinster men had acted.

War broke out shortly afterwards between the two sides and in a battle at Cúil Dremne, 3,000 of the fighting men were slain. Columba was accused of having instigated it, and being responsible for their deaths. The synod of Telltown in Meath passed a censure upon him, which would have been followed by excommunication but for the intervention of Brendan. Columba's own conscience was uneasy and by Brendan's advice, he determined to expiate himself from his offence by exiling himself from his own beloved Ireland.

This is the traditional account of the events which led to the departure of Colmcille from his own beloved country, by attempting to win for Christ as many souls as perished in the battle of Cúil Dremne. At the same time, it must be recorded, that missionary zeal and love of Christ are the only motives ascribed to him. He embarked with twelve companions in a wicker coracle and, on the eve of Pentecost, he landed on the island of Iona.

Columba in Mullach Íde

When Columcille first came to Swords in or about the year 541, he took shelter with the Gaelic chieftain in a fort now known as the fairy fort or the Ring of Malahide. He was restricted from spreading the Word of God and Christianising the people. At that time, the Druids in Swords ruled with a strong hand. Their influence spread out over a large area, where many women and children were much afraid of them, making life a misery for them. The Druids had smaller pockets of their men stationed here and there to spy for them. When they reported misdeeds as the Druids perceived them, they would come and punish the people. Columba could not make

Portrane Strand, where Finnan fought his first battle.

any advance with the pagans, so he went to his friend the chief, who advised him to go to Limerick to the warrior woman, Ita, for help. Columba agreed

Part of St. Ita's Graveyard, Malahide Portrane.

that he must go, so he set out with nine others on the long journey. Columba rode on a big bay horse and his friend was able to tell him the trouble spots to avoid.

First stop was Kildare, then Thurles, Tipperary and Charleville. On the fifth day they reached Killeedy, where Ita gave them a warm welcome and had a hot meal cooked for the weary travellers. They were able to tell Ita and her holy women their stories of the hardships and difficulties they encountered along the way.

The men gladly retired to a small sheltered compound at midday. Ita and Columcille met to discuss his problems and they

Malahide Portrane where St. Finnan had his first encounter with the Druids

talked into the night. She gave him a great deal of advice on how to handle the warring Druids and their false gods.

"You will be fighting for the glory of the Living and True God," she told them confidently, "and my prayers will be with you."

"My good Lady," replied Columcille, "I am not a fighting man and never held a sword in my hand throughout my life. I was expecting that you and your men would come to help us. I have heard many wonderful stories about you. How Jesus is your friend and is always with you."

"My holy friend," said Ita, "it is a fact of life that I cannot indulge in long journeys and battles at my age." She paused and there was a long silence. Neither one of them spoke for some time. Ita rubbed a tear from her eye and regretted that she could not spring to their help as she once would have. She had a young man who could handle such matters, but she needed him herself. He was the one she could depend on. He was her right hand man and she loved him dearly. She wondered if this was another trial, one of these situations God sends to test His holy followers. She shed some tears, but was resigned to God's will.

Finnan's qualities were many and formed him into a great and wonderful man of God. He excelled in the art of peace and could wage war when called upon to defend the good and the righteous from evil-doers. His courage and greatness of mind, as well as his ambition were not used for his own glory. His only motivation was the zeal for the glory of God. He was ranked among the most valiant and brave of the Princess's men and beat enemy forces superior in number. Now, he was embarked on an important mission and did not return for several days as he was in Itaís homeland in Waterford.

As Ita had informed him of what he should do, his mood was sad for a while. He sat beside her as she explained to him what transpired in his absence and then Ita and he decided he would leave for Malahide in three months.

*   *   *   *   *

After three full days of travel, Finnan at last arrived in Malahide on the fourth day with his ten gallant men. Columba, together with his men and the chief of Malahide were there. They took Finnan and his men to the Fort and, having rested and eaten, began to plan their campaign. They talked and went over all the proposals for three days, and, having come to a decision, they rested and prayed for four days for the success for their mission.

Finnan was given all the information, including where the outposts were and how many Druids were managing them. He was given five of Columcille's men and five of the chief's men. On the eighth day they landed in Portrane and quickly came to the Druid's post, defended by twenty-five men. Finnan told them to leave or he and his God would destroy them. Emphatically they declared that they would fight to the last man.

"Our gods are greater than yours, which we can prove," they said. They had twenty five men against Finnan's twenty, and, feeling confident in his assertions, the Druid gave the order to his men to draw swords, producing his own. He lunged towards Finnan, who stepped to one side, thrusting his own sword towards his adversary, slicing off the arm of the Druid's leader above the elbow. Somehow the sword in the severed hand rose high in the air, coming down pinning the injured man's foot to the ground. His comrades stood still as if paralysed. Finnan gave the Druids the order to leave Portrane, giving them barely enough time to gather their belongings. He stopped the bleeding of the severed arm so that the injured man might go with them.

Soon he had a church built in honour of St. Ita, staking claim to Portrane, leaving a holy man to establish the Faith.

*　　　　*　　　　*　　　　*　　　　*

Their next mission was in Donabate, another outpost where the Druids had treated the poor, down trodden people badly. Finnan's reputation was well known by now and the Druids believed that Finnan and his men were fierce and powerful warriors, with powerful Gods. Now, in Donabate, they were ready to move on as soon as the Kerry men came into sight. They had their belongings packed on mules and donkeys and moved out with great haste.

All the Druids' men in their outposts were heading for their headquarters in Swords, knowing it might be their last battle and knowing too that Finnan and his men would follow them. They thought of sending to England for help, but reinforcements would hardly get there in time at such short notice. Still they knew Finnan had only twenty men, while they had strong fortifications and a huge garrison consisting of four hundred persons. This was one of the biggest of the Druids' strongholds in Ireland, with more than one hundred qualified, experienced fighters. As the enemy could not breach the walls, the Druids could sit it out within their fortification until their foes would have to leave because of the cold and hunger. When the attackers were weak enough, they would set upon them and exact a great price in life from them.

Meanwhile, the Kerry men inspected the Druids' stronghold, to see how they were to infiltrate among these desolate men with their misdeeds and their false gods. Then they returned to the Fort in Malahide where the chief and Columba were pleased with them. They had a feast for the returned warriors and then they went back to planning for war again, which lasted for several days. Between Finnan, the Chief and Columcille, they could only muster sixty men and, under ordinary methods of fighting, this was not enough to beat the Druids. So the chief of Malahide went out to the surrounding forts to ask for help.

Meanwhile those left behind prayed to Jesus and also asked for Ita's help. The Malahide chief returned with three chiefs with over a hundred men each, which brought their force to well over three hundred, as many as could be expected and as many as were necessary. Still the fort seemed invincible. Finnan was the one with the fighting experience and Columba could come up with ideas, so they both diligently applied themselves to their various tasks.

After two weeks, the group assembled and marched to Swords. The plan which Columcille had come up with required that Finnan and his men would first go down to the wooded valley not far from the fort on the hill. They would camouflage themselves with green elder trees that grew there. Columcille, a striking figure of great stature and athletic build, with a voice so loud and melodious, it could be heard a mile off, went up to the walls of the Druid's fort

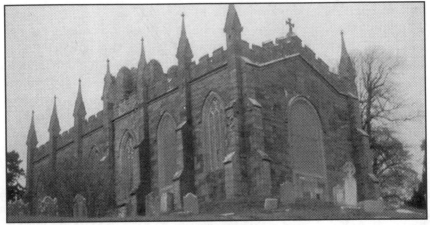
St. Columba's Church, Swords

accompanied by twenty of the most vociferous of his hundred and thirty eight men.

On reaching the fort, they shouted and roared every name under the risen sun they could think of and they ridiculed the Druids, calling them perverted, paeky, bandy legs, pluger, tormentors of women and children, badger head, hairy tail rats, goofy gods and

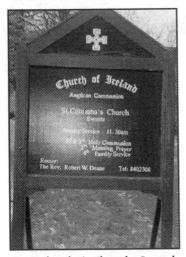
St. Columba's Church, Swords

pretentious louts. This went on for a long time and the Druids became frantic. Frustrated, their leaders got together, misconceived a plan, thinking that Finnan had only those twenty men, the same number they were informed had run them out of Portrane. They could still count that same amount of men.

"Let us make a charge against them," they said, "and we will have killed all the fools before they can even draw their swords. We will slaughter them without mercy."

Out ran the whole force of frantic Druids and, on seeing them emerge, the wily Columcille and his men turned and ran down the glen, followed by the crazy force, right into the ring of camouflaged fighting men. A mighty battle began with the ring of steel echoing around the woods and audible for miles around as swords clashed and flashed in the sunshine. Sweat and blood flowed down the Hill of Swords as the mighty fighting Druids who were expert swordsmen, met some of Finnan's men who were equally skilled. They were confused and surprised but they entered the fray with vigour and the battle raged.

Some of the Celts were young and inexperienced but their courage was admirable. Although badly wounded, they refused to lay down their swords and Finnan, the good leader that he was, shouted encouragement to them. It brought a greater effort from them, causing the Druids to draw back up the hill again.

The slaughter was great on both sides, with attack being followed by counter attack. The Druids thought by making weird noises, they could frighten the young Celts and have them hold back. Finnan's clear and mystic voice rang out loud and clear above the Druids, "Come on men, you have them beaten, one more effort will finish them." The movements were beginning to slow now and the leader of the Druids could see in a kind of mirage, his opposing leader, Finnan and thought that if he could kill him, it might swing the battle for them. This was to be his misadventure, for although he approached Finnan from behind, the Christian leader had a second sense and knew there was danger. He turned quickly and found the big Druid was almost upon him. Before the blade could come down however, a sudden spring to one side carried him from beneath it's heavy sway. Before the Druid could again swing his sword aloft, Finnan was in with a quick jab wounding his opponent. The big man had underestimated the speed and the alacrity of the youthful man he had attacked and before he could again lift his heavy sword he had received several more wounds, one under his left arm. Although the injuries were slight, he was irritated by the failure of his surprise attack and his injuries.

The fighting around him had now ended as the men on both sides lower down the hill got to hear of the private battle between the man from Kerry and the big Druid, who were battling to the finish. Some leant on their swords, while others looked on openmouthed. The clash of the steel could be heard around the evening countryside. Columba prayed to his God and to Ita, asking them to be with him and his men in their hour of need.

Once more the sturdy Druid swung his sword calling on his mighty strength, which matched his great size. He charged towards his adversary swinging his sword in a succession of artful horizontal arcs, left to right. Now with super strength, he felt he was superior to anything on earth, with all the agility and speed which that required and it took all the concentration and youthful reaction of the Waterville man to evade a storm, of which every powerful swing seemed sufficient to split solid rock.

Ita's knight was compelled to give ground before the onslaught, now backwards, now weaving from one side or the other, availing himself of the fragment of the ruins in which they were fighting. He bided his time with the utmost composure, watching all the time for when the strength of his enraged enemy might become exhausted or when by some careless or furious blow, he might expose himself to a close attack. The latter of these advantages had almost occurred, for in the middle of a headlong charge, the Druid stumbled over a large stone hidden among the long grass and before he could recover, he received a severe blow across the head from his antagonist. It landed on his Druidic bonnet, the lining of which had enclosed in it a small steel cap which saved him from serious injury, though it shocked him somewhat. Springing to his feet he renewed the battle with unabated fierceness. It seemed to Finnan, his breathing was getting more laboured, his breaths shorter. The big swordsman's blows were dealt with less strength and more caution and now, it was the Kerryman's turn to take up the attack. His light sword was easily lifted. It was easier to manoeuver, to thrust or to cut as the Druid struggled with his long, heavy sword as he lifted it with both hands. The Druid's eyes were so blood shot now that Finnan was only a vision to him. His Waterville foe began to toy with his opponent. He ripped the fastener which held the big manís cloak and it billowed backwards onto the rough ground. The fatigued leader of the Druids swung his sword once more, staggering backwards and tripping on the fallen cloak. Finnan took the advantage and quickly moved in, picking up the big sword as the Druid lay exhausted on the ground at the mercy of his opponent. Now Finnan stood like a warrior about to claim his rightful victory. He raised his sword as if to strike and heard Columba's calm voice 'Now, now, Finnan, show mercy, you are a man of God.' Finnan put his sword back in it's scabbard, giving his hand to the defeated enemy and helping him onto his feet. His foe thanked him, saying, 'Your Gods are greater than ours.'

The Druid commanded his fighters to cease fighting, but the slaughter had been great. Seventy percent of the two tribes of the young Celts were killed and Finnan alone lost twenty of his men. Most of the two tribes on the Druid's side who were left joined Columba and were converted there and then on the battlefield. Some went on to become great Christians.

Diarmuid and Ennard

Diarmuid and Ennard were two brothers and, like in many families, there was always friendly rivalry between them. Ita favoured rivalry in sports such as hunting and racing, in preparation for when boys would became warriors for their chieftain. Now they were rivals for the favours of a young girl.

Diarmuid was twenty-two and Ennard twenty years of age. The girl whom each hoped to win was eighteen. As time went by the rivalry became more intense between them, one specifying what the other should do. One day, as they argued over her, they began pushing one another. Diarmuid, being the stronger, pushed Ennard, who fell and hit his head on a stone. He lost consciousness and died that evening. A court was held and Diarmuid was accused of murdering his brother. He was found guilty within the week.

When the tragedy was reported to the fort, the Holy Women could hardly speak, remembering the two little brothers who had been brought to them by their poor mother when their father had died suddenly. She had been forced to seek Ita's help as she had had hardly enough to keep body and soul together. They remembered the happy days they had had in the classroom and the many tricks the two boys had played on them. It was sad for them to think that it had now come to this.

Ita went to her cell where she sat alone, unwilling to speak that day or break her fast. She sat there for hours, like one stunned into unconsciousness. Diarmuid's two hands had taken the life from his brother, had driven him unprepared, but more prepared than the brother who was soon to follow him to eternity. She thought then of Diarmuid's brute pride. He would keep his mouth shut, would not defend himself, but merely take whatever punishment that was meted out to him. He could never forgive himself for taking his beloved brother's life.

Then Ita thought of their mother, that little woman grieving the loss of her two sons. It was bad enough to lose their father and be left with two small boys, but now, her house was empty once again. How Itaís kind heart bled for the suffering mother, sitting all alone in her empty hovel. Seeing her helplessness finally spurred the Abbess into action. Taking one of her sisters, she left the monastery and rode to Rath where the prisoner was held in chains with two men guarding him. It was a dramatic scene, but Ita was interested only in the welfare of the prisoner. The one with a solemn face sitting on a high bench asked Ita what business had brought her to the place.

"I have come to make intercession on behalf of this condemned man," she said simply. The Chieftain looked away from the brilliant eyes which transfixed his. He was unwilling to grant her request, which was against the custom of his time and was determined to put the young man to death for this horrendous crime.

Now those around him reminded him of what the Abbess had done for him and his people many years ago when she stood up for them when they had had no one else to help them. Now the Chief hesitated, unwilling to be the first to forget her blessing. For a few moments he stayed silent, then grudgingly he told her she might have her way. She did not heed the anger in his voice and replied in measured and thankful voice.

"You have been merciful in this case and I promise you now, in the name of Christ, you too will receive mercy from Him."

The two Holy Women returned home that day. Later, Deirmaid would be sent to them, for now the Abbess was made responsible for the prisoner. Both were thinking of the consequences that might follow on what she had done and the promise she had made that day. Ita wanted her sister to tell her she had done right, that God had prompted her to ask for mercy for the young man.

Ita should not have needed the encouragement from her sister, yet the silence of the other weighed upon her, making her speak.

"He was the son of a poor widow." she said, "you cannot say I was imprudent". Still her sister said nothing. Her intervention might have been inspiration, she knew, but equally, it might have been nothing more than a kindly impulse of a kindly heart. She might face criticism from the community and from their families, or from the families for whom she had fostered children, or those who had given generously to her community.

Now the day of Diarmuid's release had arrived and it was a day which had brought her weariness and horror. She moved forward to welcome him and knelt down to unfasten his chains. She looked into his face. It was hard and impertinent and she briefly wondered about the future.

"We give him to you, Virgin of God," said the warrior leader who had accompanied him under guard. "It is our chieftain's desire that he should do penance for his crime."

Months passed and every day the Abbess visited the boy in the hut which they had given him outside the monastery. She would bring alms which some good woman had brought for him, or blackberries which had been gathered by the children. She would talk to him and give him little gifts of her own. She brought a harp that he could amuse himself with while he watched the cattle. Another time she gave him a newly woven cloak but they all lay unused in his cell.

She continued to pray for him and would not tell anyone of his continued obstinacy. She need not have kept it a secret, for all of them knew it. Some were loyal, even though they did not understand but others resented the time and care she gave to him, considering it wasted. Some went as far as to tell her that she valued his life more than theirs. By her support of the youth who had killed his brother, the monastery risked losing alms on which it depended.

The Abbess answered them all patiently and would not blame them in their complaints. She knew it would make life difficult for them if they were forsaken by the people. Still, deep down she knew she was right. Her understanding of the Christian message guided her in her compassion and, regardless of how much she needed the support and sympathy of her people, she would not give in.

She remembered Comhgán's death and the day Bishop Erc had taken her first foster son, Brendan and she realised then that her Lord would let her lean on no one but Himself. Others had taken their place, her loss and sense of loneliness was forgotten. Was it too late now to tell Christ, what she had told Him then, that she would be satisfied and more than satisfied in holding Him alone. As she told Him this in prayer, it seemed He was close again and she knew she could do all things great or small, endure great pain and be strong in His embrace.

Then she would remember Diarmuid and his dismal ways, visiting him day after day, through the hot summer. Never despair she told herself and she would try to imagine what his hurts were. He always parried her questions and would not allow her to become close to him.

One day, after bringing him some windfall apples, she spoke to him and noticed that a change of heart had come. Unable to speak, he hid his face in his hands and cried for some time, shaking all over from head to toe. He told her all his woes. He said that he had never intended to hurt even a hair on his brother's head. His heart was broken from the loss of his brother and the guilt he had suffered since. He would not defend himself and just wanted to accept all the punishment he could. Ita put her hands around him telling him she loved him as a mother and was thankful that God had spared this good young man and that she was there to play the part she had in his recovery.

A Rich Man

One day, a rich man brought a great sum of money to Ita, the self-denying servant of Christ and laid it at her feet. Ita had it removed immediately in order to show contempt for the things of this world. Ita asked her female attendants to bring water so that she could wash her hands which she felt had been in some way defiled by coming in contact with such treasure. Surprised at the action, the man asked Ita whether riches should be given to the wealthy and powerful, or to the poor and strangers. Ita considered her reply and finally replied that the treasures of the world belonged both to the rich and powerful, that they might maintain their worldly honours and to the poor and to strangers, to attain a reward in Heaven.

"What if I cannot give to both," said the man, "what am I to do then?"

"It is in your power to apply your substance in the pursuit of worldly honours, or to bestow it on the Lord," replied Ita, "for it is from Him the temporal treasure has been received and only He Hewho can accord everlasting life."

The man was greatly edified by her disinterest in wealth. He asked for and received her blessing and departed.

The spouse of Christ was accustomed to retreating frequently into some secret place, where she gave herself up entirely to prayer and Divine contemplation. She paid special attention to the mystery of the Holy Trinity, which nearly always formed the subject of her sublime meditations, and which excited devotional fervour within her soul.

"*Desirous of beholding her during these moments of transport and rapt adoration, a holy virgin stole upon her unawares and beheld three brilliant globes of light, radiant as the sun. These shed an intense and a lustrous glare over the whole space surrounding her. Alarmed at this vision, the virgin felt unable to approach St. Ita. She returned, however, filled with admiration at this unexpected apparition, which appeared emblematic of the usual subject matter occupying our saint's contemplative aspirations.*"

Killmeady Folklore

A poor couple lived near The Paps Mountains who had had seventeen children, each of whom had died at birth or shortly after. Why this had happened, nobody could tell and they searched in vain for answers. Old and wise men and women gave different reasons and gave them different remedies and instructions on how they might avoid such calamity in the future. They tried them all, but to no avail. Then, as the woman was nearing the end of her child bearing years, she went to a lonely place in the mountains where she was accustomed to going to pray. Sometimes she felt low in spirit and, during her prayers, would ask Jesus what she had ever done to to Him to merit such punishment. She would gaze at the little statue she always carried around with her and in a resigned voice would say: 'Thy will be done, O Lord'.

Then, one day, she discovered that she was going to have another child and began to fervently pray for the safe delivery of her baby.

"Little Jesus, this is the last chance for us. What can we do to save our baby?" Some nights later she had a dream in which a voice said 'There is a holy well near you, bring your baby there'. She enquired from the neighbours where this well was, but no one seemed to know. Everywhere she travelled, she asked and never paused in her search for the Holy Well.

One day, when she was in Millstreet, a wise old man told her about Ita's well. He told her many children had been cured there and told her what was required to fulfil the requirements for properly ëdoing the rounds'. She prayed fervently and, as her time for delivery came near, she made plans to bring her infant to the well of Ita. They would travel with the baby to Kilmeady as soon as it was born.

As she prepared to have the baby, the father prepared the pony and cart for travelling and, when the baby was at last delivered, they wrapped it in warm clothes and headed for Kilmeady.

When they got there, they left the road and crossed the field to the well. They took the clothes off the baby and dipped the naked infant in the cold spring water. Then the father took the baby, still naked, in his arms and jumped into the stream three times. He then ran around the ancient graveyard and stood for a few moments among the grave stones and bowed on one knee.

When he had done all that was required by the custom and tradition of the well, they wrapped the baby in his warm clothes once again, put him back in the cart and headed back home again. The mother and father were sure that God was working for them and that their baby would live. He seemed none the worse off after his morning outing, but they watched him closely in the weeks and months to follow.

They need have had no fears, for he grew up to be a strong boy and youth, who never had any sickness, not even a cold. He was good humoured and full of life and was a joy to everyone. He was so fit and healthy that it was said he had got life from his sisters and brothers who had died and perhaps some from Ita as well.

Tur na Foladh

Near St. Ita's well is a stone which is said to bear the impression of Itaís favourite donkey. The beast was used for the purpose of bringing new milk to the convent for her people, from the land on which she kept cows and grew crops to feed her community. It was a four mile journey and the donkey went back and forth each day without any guide. When ready, the milk was put in two pails which hung like panniers on either side of the faithful beast. On one occasion, robbers who made a raid on the farm, found the donkey with the two pails of milk ready to make the return journey. The raiders were so enraged at not finding any treasure as expected, that they overturned the pails of milk and let it flow down the hillside. The anger of God was upon them immediately, for He turned that milk which was intended to support Ita and her household and which would also be distributed among the needy and the poor, into blood. Some of the blood was on the clothes of the raiders and, that night while they slept at their campsite, the wolves came from the nearby wood and killed them. That is how the townland and parish was given the name of Tura na Fuileac which in English means abundance of blood.

On another occasion, the donkey stood on a large thorn which entered the sole of its hoof, making it badly lame. Ita pulled out the thorn which she thrust into the ground, at the same time commanding it not to lame the donkey again. It then grew into a large tree and that whitethorn was unique in that all the thorns pointed downwards. It grew up into the shape of a cross and flourished until recent times, when the surface around it was disturbed and so Ita's thorn tree withered and died. This was in existence up to twenty years ago, but is no longer available as an object of veneration.

Conformed to Christ on the Cross

For years, St. Ita suffered from a mysterious pain in her side, so grievous that she could hardly walk upright. The cause of this is not known and it may be that it was a mystical grace, a sharing like that which Padre Pio had in the pain of the Crucifixion, or what St. Margaret Mary would frequently experience on a Friday.

Neverthless, Ita would not allow this pain to lessen her desire to do penance. Some of her contemporaries used a pillow of wood, some even of stone, while St. Ita, from the time she left the Decies, never used a pillow at all. In this respect they were perhaps a different race from us; but not, let us hope, in our love of prayer or devotion to the Virgin's Son. Despite the hard life, St. Ita lived to a very great age.

Ailbhe Is Shown the Light

The Abbess was in her cell one day with Ailbhe, a novice who had entered the monastery not many weeks before. The girl had spoken little since she came to Cluain Credail, too intent, it seemed, on the call she heard within. Now the Abbess was reading to her from a copy of St. John's Gospel.

"He will come," she read, "and it will be for Him to prove the world wrong about sin, about judgment and about righteousness of heart." She stopped and looked at the other to see if she understood, but the novice was no longer listening, and Ita realised that she had been talking to a stranger. The girl's soul was shut to her. She waited, then asked of Christ, the grace to help in some way this virgin whom she now saw to be cut off from the light that shone so gloriously in her own mind.

"You are not at peace, mo leana," the Abbess said. "You have not found happiness in Cluain Credail."

Ailbhe looked at her as she had so often done during the past weeks. It was not easy to tell her the cause of her discontent, the temptation to envy she had felt from the first days she had experienced the holiness, the youthful wisdom and the beauty of the Abbess of Cluain Credail. She worked miracles, they said, and gave counsel to kings, yet Ailbhe, who also had sacrificed her virginity to Christ, who also had left a royal home and put on coarse clothing, had had no favour granted her, no glimpse of Paradise.

It was difficult to reveal so petty a sin, but she would know no peace until she did. What David said is true of each of us. 'While I kept my own secret all day long, I cried to Thee in vain...' Like him she became her own accuser, and told the Abbess of the jealousy that ate at her soul.

"Why does God love you so," she asked, "more than He loves any other of His virgins?"

The Abbess was startled by the confidence she had heard and by the question that followed it, but her expression revealed nothing but a readiness to listen, and seeing this, Ailbhe asked her question after question, all that she had stored in her mind during the silent weeks.

"You have healed the sick," she said, "you have knowledge of the future; the evil spirits fear you, they say . . . . . they even say you have spoken with an angel of God and received bread from his hands. I have watched you in prayer and I see that you cling without any distraction to the most Holy Trinity. How did you come by such grace? What is your secret? What can I do to be as you are?"

The young Abbess raised her right hand to sign the girl's forehead with a Cross, a very Celtic gesture and as she did, she made her reply.

"You answered your own question," she said, "when you told me that I pray always to the Three Divine Persons. Whoever does this, recollecting herself, and holding conversation in her heart with the Blessed Trinity, will have God close always; and if I possess these powers you speak of, it is only because of the union I have with Him who can do all things."

The young holy woman was silent for a few moments. Suddenly she smiled; the mountain of pain and penance she had thought to lie between her and her King had melted like wax before Ita's words and instead of its dark bulk, she saw before her the road of familiar, easy love where the saints walk.

The answer given to Ailbhe by her Abbess was for her the revelation, showing how Ita had turned over in her mind the rebuke given to her by the Angel. She could have told Ailbhe of her fasts and cross-vigils, penances that would always lure her, but she did not; she told her instead to talk to God in her heart.

The Death of Ita,
Princess, Virgin and Holy Woman

As she grew older and her movements got slower, Ita, with a lifetime of the Lord's work behind her, began to spend more and more time in her Chapel. Unable to be out and about ministering to her people, she would look back on her life, her work for Christ, her battles with the Druids, the difficulties of her childhood and youth and take some satisfaction in what she had achieved. As a perfectionist and as one dedicated solely to the work of the Lord, she would often wonder if she could have achieved more for Christ and for her people; could have fed and clothed more, could have brought the Good News to more of those who had never heard of her One, True God and who thirsted for justice.

Now, Ita sat in the dark little chapel, close as she could to the Blessed Sacrament and closed her eyes. She seemed always to be tired now. Breathing was difficult and caused a stabbing pain in her side. She thought of Christ trying to breathe on the Cross and would offer up her discomfort for her sons, the way He did for all his children on earth. She went over their names and what a litany they made. Brendan, Fachtna, Mochoemog and all the others, and now there was Cumméne. She thought too, of her spiritual sisters. It was in this chapel that they had vowed to maintain their virginity for Christ. Such numbers of them, all remembered and all loved. She recalled her first companions, buried now in the shadow of the oratory. Emer was there and Blánaid and Tireen and Eannaigh. Surely she could say of Cluain Credail what Ciarán had said of Clonmacnois: 'Many souls will ascend to Heaven from this place'. What a glorious thought that made, but it did not make her any less lonely. She wished she could see them again, the saints she had known long ago, but all were dead. Erc and Comhgán, Luchtigern and Lasrain; her sons she knew were scattered throughout the Kingdoms of Ireland and even beyond its seas. Brendan was ruling his great abbey at Clonfert; Mochoemog had left home many months ago with the bell she had given him for the day he would found a school of his own, and Fachtna the Eloquent lay buried now at Ros Alithir, beneath the great monastery he had built there.

Now, as she sat in front of the Blessed Sacrament, she spoke directly to her Lord.

"I am getting too old," she told Christ suddenly and wearily, "too old and tired. When will You come for me?"

The days grew shorter and bitterly cold and so keen were the winds on Christmas night that her Prioress begged her to stay in her cell until it was time for Mass. She would come herself then, she promised, to bring her to the chapel.

The Abbess lay there, wrapped warmly but without the support of a pillow. 'I haven't used one since I left the Decies', she said crossly, 'and I'm not going to use one now'. So they allowed her to have her way.

Alone, her mind went back to Cumméne, as it had done so often these last weeks, and a great longing to see him brought tears to her eyes. He would soon be vesting for Mass, she knew, at Ardfert's high altar. How she wished he could say Mass here instead and let her receive her last Christmas Holy Communion from him and not from a stranger. "Cumméne," she whispered "Cumméne, a mhic," and her eyes closed.

Midnight came and the Prioress returned as she had promised to bring the Abbess to Mass. "Mother," she called softly, then seeing that she was asleep, she left her, closing the door noiselessly behind her. After Mass she returned, and sat by Ita's bedside in case she should wake and ask for Holy Communion. Ita sensed her presence and opened her eyes. They were grey and clear, thought the Prioress, as they had always been. 'The priest is waiting' she told her, 'to bring you Holy communion if you wish for It'.

"I've had Holy Communion," the aged Holy Woman replied. "I knelt just now in the porch of Cumméne's church in Ardfert and my son came down from the altar to give me the Body of my Lord Jesus Christ."

"What a beautiful dream!" thought the Prioress, as she left again. But the Princess Ita knew that it was not a dream. She knew it meant that Christ who loved her with an everlasting love, wanted to prepare her by that Holy Communion for their final embrace. He would come very soon, she told herself, the rider on the white horse, the Faithful and True, the Christ Child she had petted in every child she had held. She thought He might come for her on the day of His Circumcision, or on the great feast of His Epiphany, but she lingered on through the first days and weeks of January.

They asked her to pray for her friend Aengus, Abbot of Clonmacnoise, who was sick. Messengers were on their way, they told her, to fetch him water blessed by her hands. "I'll bless the water now," she said, "for I'll not live to greet his monks. But warn them that it cannot help, for Aengus will die before they return. Poor monks, their Abbot will be in Heaven and they still on the road."

Once on a visit to Clonmacnoise, Ita received the Eucharist from a very holy priest without it being known who she was. After her departure her true identity was discovered. Immediately the priest with other members of the order set out for Ita's retreat house in order to receive her blessing. On the way, one of the men lost his sight, but it was restored by Ita when they reached her sanctuary.

*   *   *   *   *

When it was recognized that Ita's final days were drawing to a close, word was sent out to her foster sons and those she had tutored to come to Killeedy. All who were able to come, came with no hesitation or delay. Cumméne came from Ardfert, Finbarr from Cork, Finnan from Malahide, Luchtigern from Inistymon and Mochoemog from Thurles.

As they arrived, she greeted each one separately. Wearily, but yet very interested, she wanted to know how all her people were faring, what churches they had built and how many people had joined their Christian religion. She thought of all her holy sons, who, in all must amount to several hundred. She wondered where Brendan was. She could visualise him as a mere baby. She could hear him laugh and cry and felt she could sense him coming to her. How she loved him; Brendan, her first foster son followed by Fachtna the Eloquent, then Comhgán, her sons. She knew they had scattered throughout the Kingdom of Ireland and even beyond the seas. She remembered the hurling games in which she was sometimes asked to keep the peace. She could remember the noise when one side or the other scored. The Memories began to tire her and she closed her eyes to rest.

A little later, she asked for Holy Viaticum and when it was done, her Holy Sisters came to her to receive her last kiss. At the gates, the men and women of Uí Connaill crowded around, begging that they might come to her and all were received.

Late that day, when the priests and people of the kingdom had gone and the dying Abbess was left alone with her nuns, the Prioress asked her to appoint her successor, promising in the name of all, that they would give their allegiance to the Holy Woman she chose.

"No woman will succeed me as Abbess," was the mysterious reply, but so low and weak was her voice that some wondered if those were indeed her words. Others, seeing the expression of pain on her face, were reminded of Christ crying out that He was forsaken by His Father, and asked themselves if she too, believed her life′s work to have been rejected. Her pain was pitiful to see and it was with tears that her daughters took up the antiphon for the departing soul. At last, her expression seemed to relax and they knew the struggle was almost over.

As she relaxed into near sleep, she wondered to herself, when Christ would come for her. Opening her eyes briefly, she asked everyone to leave her alone to be with Christ. Later, a great blaze was seen in Ita's cell and her Holy Sisters rushed to her, fearing she was caught in a fire. They stopped in their tracks, for all they could see were three balls of fire floating above her. They withdrew, knowing it was the holy fire of the Lord; God's fire, welcoming her towards Heaven.

In her mind, Ita was young again, catching up Íosagán in her arms and seeing through His eyes the Eternal and Triune God.

It was the fifteenth day of January, about the year A.D. 556.

St. Ita's Grave at Killedy, Co. Limerick

The End

Tubrid, Well of Ita

Tubrid waters crystal clear;
A Grotto and an Altar near.
Well of Ita of the Gael,
Waters never known to fail.
How fitting that those waters be
Surrounded by a Rosary.

The Story of Ita's Hymn

Perhaps it was during peacetime that Ita first held in her arms the little prince of peace. She was at prayer when, just as he had done in her youth, God sent her an angel and once again, Mithiden stood before her. He asked her what reward she would like for her prayers, her fasting, her hard work and her penance.

"Tell the son of the Virgin," replied Ita, "that I want one grace. Let me hold Iosagán in my arms. Let me foster the son of God here in my cell." The angel left her and Ita held in her arms Prince Iosagán and as she held the child, Ita was imagining herself in the place of Mary and trying to understand her and share in her joys and sorrows. Certainly, Ita's closeness to Jesus and Mary have been the secret of her work. The devotion of the people of Munster to her is not an extravagance, but something deeply rooted in their affection for her.

Ísuchán

Alar lium im disíurán;
Cia beith cléirech co lín sét
Is bréch uile acht Ísucán.

Altram alar lium, im thig,
Ní altram nach dóerathaig-
Ísu co feraib nime,
Frim chride cech n-óenadaig.

Ísucán óc mo bithmaith;
Ernaid, ocus ní maithmech.
In Rí con-ic na uilí
Cen a guidi bid aithrech.
Ísu úasal ainglide,
Noco cléirech dergnaide,
Alar lium im disirtán.
Ísu mac na Ebraide.

Maic na ruirech, maic na rig,
Im thir cía do-ísatán,
Ní uaidib saílim sochor,
Is tochu lium Ísucán.

Canaid cóir, a ingena
Dífir dliges bar císucán;
Atá'na phurt túasucán
Cía beith im ucht Ísucán.

It is Iosagan who is nursed
By me in my little hermitage
Though a cleric have great wealth
It is all deceitful save Iosagán

The nursing done by me in my
House is no nursing of a base churl;
Jesus with Heaven's inhabitants
Is against my heart every night.

Iosagán óg is my lasting good;
He never fails to give.
Not to have entreated the King.
Who rules all will be a cause of sorrow.

It is noble angelic Jesus
And no common cleric
Who is nursed by me
In my little hermitage
Jesus, Son of the Hebrew Woman.

Though prince's sons and king's sons
Come into my country-side
Not from them do I expect profit;
I love Iosagán better.

Sing a choir-song, maidens
For Him to Whom your tribute is due,
Though Iosagán be in my bosom,
He is in His mansion above.

Appendix 1
A Prayer to St. Ita

St. Ita,
We come to you each day and night,
And pray to you by candlelight,
Come to us in your virginity
Show us a sample of your reality.

Come to us each day;
Guide us on our way
Bring to us those great Spirits
The Blessed Trinity.

Let us beckon to all mankind
And leave our troubles far behind.
Come to us each day
In our work and in our play.

When we lay our weary heads
Down to sleep upon our beds;
If we die before we wake,
Our souls to God we pray you take.

When we go before our judge
Ask for him to grant to us
Pardon, absolution and
Remission of all our sins
And give to us everlasting life.
Amen.

J.D.

Gather Up the Fragments

Gather up the fragments lest they be lost. In St. John's Gospel, 6, 12 these words inspired me to pick up the threads of the story of what made Irishmen and women a Christian community in cities and rural villages in Ireland. We have had many great saints, from outside Ireland and many native Irish saints especially in Munster. Sadly most are gone from memory and tradition and are forgotten. The same applies to our Waterford Saints and the one who stands out most in my mind is St Declan of Ardmore. There are three Kilmeaden Saints; Ita who is buried in Killeedy, Co. Limerick; St. Eannaigh buried in Ardfert near Tralee, Co. Kerry and St Mochoemog buried in Thurles, Co. Tipperary. It would be sad however if we lost all sense of our past.

ARDFERT

This collection of memories brings together, not in any order or sequence, stories of one aspect of our glorious past. We had young men and women with high ideals; with faith and courage, ready to leave kith and kin, home and homeland to spread the gospel, thus changing the lives of more people in near and far off lands.

Three more Waterford priests I would like to mention are: Doctor Edward Barron, Clonea, Rathgormack, known as the unsung hero of the mission to Africa b.1801 - died 1854 in Savannah, USA. The Barron Family donated the stained glass window in the church in Clonea, which was dedicated to our Saint Ita, in 1901, this window displaying the Barron Crest was to serve as a memorial to the Barron Family of Ballyneale, Co. Waterford Next, Michael McGrath b. 1808 Ballyristeen, Kill and Richard Walsh Ballyvadden, Kill, b. 1814. These men were the first missionary priests to the Catholic Church in Australia. One writer described the place as hell abandoned.

There were no fences and only wagon tracks marked the travellersí course through the bush. The priest set out on horse back, the sacred vestments strapped to the saddle. In this fashion he passed from station to station. The territory covered by Rev. McGrath in his missionary duties consisted of over 10,000 square miles. His health, like so many of the clergy of that time and place, soon deteriorated and he returned to Co. Waterford. He lived alone in his cottage in Benvoy, Annestown and died in 1893 aged 85 years. His grave stone stands beside Dunhill church. Fr. Walsh died at his home in Ballyvadden, Kill in 1868, aged 54 years. His plaque is on the wall of the little church in Faugheen, Kill. They were great ambassadors for God and for Ireland and we should never let them be forgotten.

Ita's Suffering

The Holy Woman St. Ita, it is said, suffered a bodily affliction, which she carefully concealed from the knowledge of others. It was said to contain something like a big beetle-like worm, getting bigger as time went on. It is now believed that it was some form of cancer. The saint denied herself many comforts in her unrelenting effort to live in the presence of God, with faithfulness to the people of Munster and of Ireland.

She called all her loved ones around her and told them in a calm voice that her term or sojourn of life was coming to an end. Like Joan of Arc, Ita in her day, fought the Druids and freed the people from slavery. Now, as she prepared to leave this life, she recalled the vision her father had seen in her youth in Kilmeaden. He had seen three great Spirits welcoming her into Heaven, dressed as a Celtic Warrior and leading many souls to God. This she had done throughout her life. She had fought for, and with her spouse, Jesus. Now those Spirits were coming for her to bear her to her home in heaven.

Statue of St. Ita in Raheenagh Church Killeedy.

Tradition says that it was on a Friday that Ita died, the day of the week on which our Saviour gave His life for us and that she commended her soul to the King of all Fridays, whose body was stretched and nailed to the cross. She breathed out her soul in an act of pure love, with no one by her side, as she went to her Heavenly Spouse and her King. This Holy Virgin, having led a life of great purity, died on the 15th day of January. Her Holy Women and all her

Holy Men, her foster sons and all the people from the countryside all about, crowded around to bid her a last farewell.

St. Ita's church stands at the back of the ruins where her statue stands today, which is on the site of an early settlement. She was buried on the right hand side, near the entrance to her own church. The second part of the building, where her statue stands, was added later.

From the list of early monasteries, it would be easy to get the impression that there were very few convents. We know that women were equally drawn to religious life as men, if not more so. This was probably due to the fact that by an old Irish law, women were only allowed a life-long interest in the ownership of land and, on their death, it would revert to a male. This could be the reason why St. Ita's Abbey was occupied by monks and not by Holy Women after the saint's death. This law would have considerably reduced the number of nunneries all over the country.

Extract from the poem
"Vale, Fr. Pat" by John O'Brien

We turned our horses' heads out west, beyond the farthest track,
With nothing but an alien star to light the journey back.
The echoes mocked us as we went, and silence startled sat
When out beyond the rim of things we marched with Father Pat.
We said our Mass in canvas tents, and 'neath the gnarled trees;
Of red-gum slabs and sheets of bark we built our sanctuaries;
Our axes rang on timbered slopes above the mining flat,
And church and school and convent mark the path of Father Pat.

**(John O'Brien was the nom-de-plume
of Australian Catholic priest Father Patrick Joseph Hartigan (1878-1952),
who was Parish Priest of Narandera NSW, Australia for 27 years.**

Some Background on the Druids

The Druids were a religious group found in Ireland, England, Scotland, Wales and France and were established by the Jews who evangelised many parts of Europe including these islands. They were very active around the time of the Exodus, when they spread around Europe questing for food. We know that they also arrived in Ireland and established an order among the tribes here. Their religious practices changed over the years until they ended up as what we call the Druids.

There is reference in Irish history to leaders who came from as far away as Spain and while they were known to be Milesians, they were also Jews.

The Druids still existed around 400AD, but were being diminished by the growth of Christianity. They were almost wiped out in those parts of Europe dominated by the Romans because they were very much against the God worshipped by the Jews and later the Christians.

Druids were very interested in old Jewish astrology, the promotion of agriculture and the sowing of seed etc. They were highly educated and very secretive like the Sanhedrin of two thousand years ago, who kept much of the teaching to themselves. They were sworn to secrecy in many things. They had also inserted some of their own beliefs developed over the years into the Jewish religion to become what we know as the Druids.

After a while, due to the distance between them and the change in some of their beliefs, they became cut off from Jerusalem. It is said, though there is no proof, that they also practised human sacrifice.

They followed the movements of the sun and moon and practised their agriculture according to what they learned there. The Jewish religion and many other religions go by the same principles today.

The influence of the Druids was as much social as it was religious. Druids not only took the part which modern priests would, but were often the philosophers, scientists, lore-masters, teachers, judges and counsellors to the kings. The Druids linked the Celtic peoples with their numerous gods, the lunar calendar and the sacred natural order. With the arrival of Christianity in each area, all these roles were assumed by the bishop and the abbot.

Druidic lore consisted of a large number of verses learned by heart, and we are told that sometimes twenty years were required to complete the course of study. Of their oral literature of sacred songs, formulas for prayers and incantations, rules of divination and magic, not one verse has survived, even in translation, nor is there even a legend that we can call purely Druidic, without a Christian overlay or interpretation.

MEMORIES OF KILBARRYMEADEN FOLKLORE FROM NEDDY 'NAILER' CASEY

In the year 2000, I spoke to Neddy 'Nailer' Casey who lived all his life in the area and asked him if he knew any folklore about St. Ita in Kilbarrymeaden.

"Well," said Nailer modestly, "I have forgotten most of what my dear father told to me. However, I do remember coming home from school in our bare feet. We would feel the heat from the road on our scarred feet and we would walk up and down the stream to soothe them after a long hot day."

He then told me they would elect someone to be St. Ita, which would be a great honour. The chosen one would have great power, as the rest fought her as Druids. She would stand with a long stick in her hand and knock down the one who would dare to stand against her. All would lay still for a few minutes, then she would say magic words. Everyone would come to life as she touched them in turn. Then they would say, 'Sorry Princess' bow and say thank you.

"Ah well," said Nailer, "that brings memories back to me of hearing my father talk about the Holy Woman, as he used to call her. He used to talk about the fishermen and how she often saved them from the cruel seas and kept away the evil spirits. He spoke of all the cures they had at her Holy Well, the many people who came from the city of Waterford, looking for peace and contentment.

Yes, he used to tell us St. Ita was reputed to have been born between the last hour of April and the first hour of May. That time of year was somewhat early for a Pattern, so for whatever reason, they chose the 27th of July for her Pattern day. It usually started with a half day of celebrations on Saturday and would finish on Sunday night, when a big fire burned at Kill Beg cross, not far from St. Ita's Well. There would be dancing round the fire after a great day of sporting activities.

Kilbarrymeadan

On the hill called Manacaun, stood St. Ita's church and graveyard. The church measured fifty feet by twenty, with no altar, just a crude cross with a figure of Jesus on it, hanging by chains from the roof. It was said, when St. Ita knelt before it, tears flowed from her eyes. Nicky Power, who lives near the road at the bottom of the hill, says his mother told him it used to be called the Holy Hill of St. Ita.

The site of St. Ita's Church and graveyard, Kilbarrymeadan.

Ancient Church Crucifix

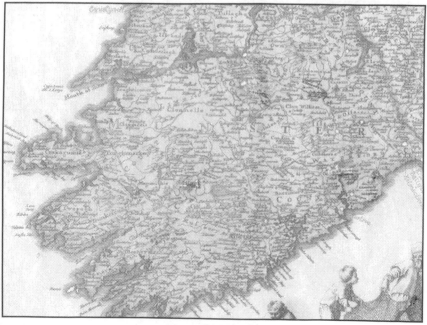

Map of Munster

His brother wondered how anybody could dig a grave on the rock up on that hill. Nicky maintains that this is incorrect, as the graveyard extended out into the next field where it is not as rocky. His mother also told him St. Ita had a school before she travelled out on her missions. Below the road a college was built, where many were taught to become Holy Men, including some druids who brought the Word of God back to England and Cornwall. Long after all signs of that college had disappeared, crops sown there were known to fail. One person who thought he had succeeded in growing a crop of potatoes, found that when they were put in a pot they melted into the water.

The Story of Gortroe Church
A Commitment unfulfilled since the time of St. Ita

Early one morning, Hannah O'Neill grandmother of Ita O'Neill, had a dream, a vision about St. Ita. Many centuries ago, their ancestor and his people had lost their lives in a battle in Gortroe defending the young Ita from the 'Mad Prince'. Now, Ita, the Warrior Princess, wanted a church and school built on the site of the battlefield.

In the morning before rising, Hannah O'Neill made her husband promise he would do all in his power to carry out the saint's wishes and make them known to the people of Clonpriest and the surrounding area. Everybody agreed that as a people they should give it their best effort. Where was the money to come from, now that times were poor? God and St. Ita would provide when the time came, they said. So be it.

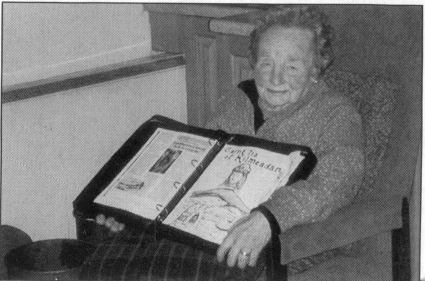

Ita O'Neill on First
Communion Day

Ita Vaughan O'Neill

Ita O'Neill today

The first meeting was held at the very spot where Ita's uncle had fallen and it was decided they would go to Lord Ponsonby and ask him for a site. He was amenable towards the proposal and not only did he provide a site, he donated some money to start the effort going. It was suggested that anybody with relations in America should contact them and ask them to raise funds for their church too.

Most had relations in Boston, so some of the emigrants went to the Bishop there to ask for permission to raise funds. He promised he would speak to his people. One such emigrant was Seán O'Donnacadha, from Killbarrymeaden. He came from a parish and townland where St. Ita was well known and had a job as a foreman in a construction company. Not only did the Corkmen subscribe at his request, so also did the rest of the Munster men who worked for that great company.

After two years or more, he had a significant amount of money raised, but now his troubles began. He had many begging letters from churches in Boston and his own county Waterford. His sister and her husband told him he should send money home to his mother and orphan daughter. He even got threats to hand over the money to some undesirables. The honourable man that he was, he refused to bow to any of the requests to him and he sent the money home with a trustworthy man from Gortroe whose father had died.

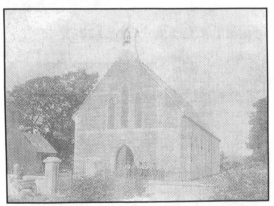

The proceeds of his two years work were sent in paper form and only three men knew the money was coming, one of whom was John O'Neill, Ita O'Neill's grandfather, the others a priest and a family connection.

An old photo of St. Ita's Church, Gortroe

When the work began, help came from all quarters. All the farmers gave a horse and cart and there were several stonemasons among the locals. When they had not got a man for a particular job, men came from Cork city and farther afield. There were special men for the many specialised jobs and they never asked for payment. The women looked after the welfare of the men and there were many romances made in Gortroe at that time. John O'Neill was foreman and he devoted all his time to building St. Ita's church. It was finished in 1907, eight years after the Virgin Ita appeared to

Hannah O'Neill. A beautiful stained glass window which was donated by Hannah and her husband John depicts our saint Ita and there is also an inspiring picture of St. Ita measuring 6ft by 4ft, which was presented by a young girl, Kate O Neill. It cost the significant sum of five pounds at that time.

ITA VAUGHAN-O'NEILL

Ita Vaughan-O'Neill was born in 1907, the same year as the church was built in Gortroe. When she was born two priests came to her

father and asked him if he would give her the name Ita in honour of the Saint and the Church of the Parish. It is said that Ita's grandmother, Hannah O'Neill had a vision of St. Ita in which she asked for a church to be built.

Now, ninety-eight years after the Church was dedicated, Ita is looking forward to being there for its Centenary in two years time and taking an active part in the celebrations.

Kate O'Neill's present to Gortroe
Church. The picture cost £5.

Scoil Íte, Patrick's Hill, Cork

**The Plaque in Cork which marks the site of Scoil Íte
in Patrick's Hill, Cork City.**

After her early release from prison and her dismissal from her teaching job, Máire nic Shuibhne, sister of Terence Mac Swiney, Lord Mayor of Cork, sent for her sister, Eithne, who was teaching in a Benedictine School in the Isle of Wight and, inspired by Padraig Pearseís school, St. Enda's, which has been described as 'the miracle of a school in Ireland, more truly Irish than any that had existed in the country since The Flight of the Earls,' she founded Saint Ita's High School and Kindergarten in Cork.

The school was opened on September 4th 1916, with the primary aim of inspiring pupils with a love, loyalty and pride in the heritage of their land and language. Helped by loyal friends, they put Scoil Íte on a firm foundation. In Scoil Íte, pupils were prepared for the matriculation and the entrance examination of the National University.

The only serious handicap in those early years was the absence of the Mac Swiney sisters during the long drawn out agony of Brixton when Mary and Eithne were attending their brother during his hunger strike. But even then the work went on without interruption in the school where Terence MacSwiney had himself once taught.

In the art of teaching, Máire and Eithne Mac Swiney seemed inspired. They understood the individual child as few people can do and the closure of their school on Thursday 17th June 1954 brought to an end a glorious chapter in Irish education.

Colaiste Íde, Dingle, Co. Kerry

Recollections of Clonpriest Schooldays
As narrated by Ita Vaughan O'Neill
A Nonagenarian born August 1907

"Mary and I went to school together," said Ita. Clonpriest was a four-teacher school, male and female. Mr. Millerick was principal of the boys' school and Mr. William Supple was the assistant. Miss Pyne was principal of the girls' school and Miss Hanley was her assistant. There were ninety-three girls on roll and approx. the same number of boys. In fact with the large families then, there were a hundred children living between "Ceann an Bhothair" - Redbarn strand and Gortroe village.

A high wall divided the boys from the girls. There was grass around the edges where trees grew also. The playground was covered with gravel. Behind the playground and school, where the "bush" is now, there was a vegetable garden where lessons on horticulture were given. There was also a flower garden on the plot. This was part of the children's education. The boys and girls alike worked in the plot with their teachers. Every girl wore a white pinafore. This was bought at Merricks. From time to time these were inspected by the inspector. Ita recalls a day when the pinafores were being inspected. Minutes before it, she got her pinafore caught in the desk and put a triangular tear on it. When the inspection was taking place, she was hauled out and vehemently rebuked for having torn her pinafore. There were no questions asked as to when or how it happened.

Catechism and handwriting were very important to Miss Hanley. The religious and other inspectors were rather severe in those times.

There was no Irish taught during school hours, but after school, Irish was taught for a half an hour. This was optional.

Children were kept in after school to tidy up. They were also kept in, as punishment was meted out.

During potato picking, children were kept at home, without question. Families helped, cousins also.

Ita recalls a day when she fadged. She drank her bottle of milk and ate her lunch up the boreen. Alas! she got caught. There was nothing said, but she was sent picking potatoes and denied dinner that evening. Her rumbling stomach reminded her that fadging wasn't very wise after all.

Ita and the rest of her family walked two miles to and from school. There were two girls kept in every evening after school to sweep the school. The teacher set and lit the fire in the morning.

On wet days, the horse or pony would be tackled and the children would be ferried to school. Play consisted of skipping, hopscotch, "tig" and dancing in the corner. The boys kicked football. Even though life was hard, the children were quite happy. They were memorable days for Ita.

(From "Clonpriest National School - 100 Years, 1902 - 2002" published by Gortroe Centenary Committee)

Kilmead, Co. Kildare

The lands of Kilmead were in the ownership of the Fitzgerald family. As a result at the Rebellion of Silken Thomas 1534, the land passed to Martin Pelles as a reward to his loyalty during the suppression of the Geraldine rebellion. He was also given constableship of Athy. The Church of St. Joseph, Ballymount was erected by Archdeacon Brady during the years 1876 - 1878. The Church of St. Ita, Kilmead was built about 1798. It is believed the site was donated by the Kenna family who were the relatives of Cardinal Paul Cullen. Both churches are of cruciform design. While travelling from the direction of St. Ita's Park and facing the front of the Church, there are four strong stone columns visible. These are situated on the roof of the church and resemble four cannons. The graveyard in Kilmead is the burial place of the Fitzgerald family with graves existing from the 17th century and earlier. Among those buried there is Thomas Fitzgerald who died March 28th 1835. He was landlord of the area. His sisters Anne and Elizabeth, who left a handsome bequest to the Sisters of Mercy in Athy, were also buried there.

(From St. Ita's Church, Kilmead Bi-centenary, 1798 - 1998)

The people of this area have great devotion to St. Ita, believing that through their prayers and supplications to her, she helped them through the darkest days of Famine Ireland.

Two plaques are erected in the Parish, one of which recalls the life of St. Ita and the other commemorates the Bicentenary of the Parish Church of St. Ita.

St. Finnan established a church here, one of about eight he founded in or near Dublin. This he dedicated to St. Ita.

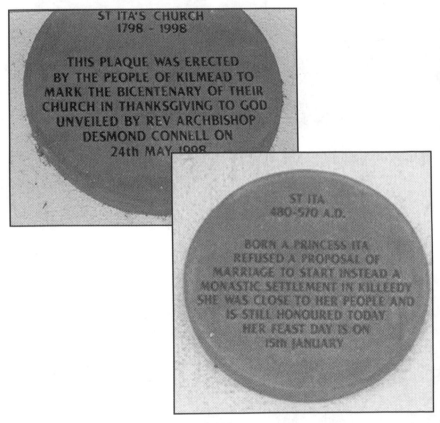

Kilmead
Church,
Co. Kildare

St. Ita's Park
in Kilmead

ST ITAS PARK
PAIRC NAOMH IDE

Tombs of the
Fitzgerald
Clan,
Kilmead,
Co. Kildare

Tobar Neantoga

Bruno Donoghue, schoolmaster and historian in the early 19th century, researching with the school children and their parents, confirmed the folklore regarding St. Ita's time in Killeedy, Crossbarry. The well is called Tobar Neantóga, or the Well of the Nettles. Ita used to boil nettles and local herbs with water from the well and many people with various illnesses were cured. These had to be taken only in the month of May. To this day, these nettles are used in the same way, in the hope of cures.

Ita's Well - Kilmeedy, Cork

There are many tales in the folklore of St. Ita and her cures. One such tells the story of a little girl who was born with a short leg, so badly deformed that she was unable to walk. One day, her father put his daughter on his back, took her to Ita's well on three consecutive days and went around the ancient graveyard which surrounded the well. Each day he took off his shoes and jumped into the water.

On one such visit, he left his daughter by the stream and went to a nearby field to make hay. When he returned, the girl was nowhere to be seen. This worried him greatly so he hurried home. When he arrived there, the little girl had arrived before him and smiled at

him and ran into his arms. She had walked all the way home on her own, fully cured.

St. Ita's Well, Kilmeedy, Millstreet

Slánan (Slánann)

The following was related by Mr. John O'Leary, a farmer of Kilmeedy, Millstreet, Co. Cork, Aged 70 years.

The Slánan is situated in the most eastern part of the townland of Kilmeady, about a mile and a half from Millstreet. It consists of a Holy Well dedicated to the Blessed Virgin and St. Ita and a burial ground where many of those who died in the neighbourhood during the famine years were buried. There being only one coffin to be had in those desperate times, this was used to take the bodies to the graveside and was then taken back for the next corpse, while the one that was brought would be buried in the holy ground wrapped in whatever meagre covering was available, or without a shroud at all.

Ancient Stone Church

A very efficacious round is performed at this blessed well and it is the custom in the neighbourhood to perform it for any bodily ailment. Practically everyone in the locality can testify to some personal cure, and cures have repeatedly taken place on a promise to do this round.

Kneeling at the entrance to the well, beside the white thorn tree which grows on its western brink, the round is started. First an offering is made of the round in honour of Our Lady and the Saint of the well, for the desired cure, or in thanksgiving for a cure already effected, on promise of this round. Still kneeling, the person recites seven Paters, Aves and Glorias and then starts the Rosary. Rising to his feet on commencing the first decade, he walks very slowly round the well, by the left, where there is a clearly defined path until he returns to the spot from whence he started.

Having now recited a decade or more of the rosary, he kneels and says again the Seven Paters, Aves and Glorias. He then rises, follows the same path as before and continues the rosary. Returning to the entrance to the well, he again kneels on the spot as before and recites a third time the Seven Paters, Aves and Glorias. On rising, he continues the rosary following the same path as before and on coming to the place from whence he started, he finishes the rosary.

He then takes some water from the well and bathes his hands and also any affected part if the body. Next, he gets more water from the well and takes three drinks in honour of the Blessed Trinity.

The days for the round are Thursday, Friday and Saturday of any week in the year, but it must be done on the three consecutive days and it is necessary to hear Mass on the Sunday following in order to complete the round.

Many articles of devotion are left at the well, as it is a custom that everyone making the round should leave something on the final day. Over the well is a Crucifix and printed on it are the words 'Lord hear my prayer and let my cry come unto Thee'

What is known as the 'Long Round' is made in the same manner on twenty one consecutive days, starting on a Thursday. The 'Short Round' is then added on the last three days of the week making twenty four rounds in all.

The owner of the farm (Mr. Meaney) in which the well is situated, built a room of his dwelling-house on the passage leading to the well and the roof was blown off every time it was put on. Noises were heard in the room and finally, it was decided not to occupy it at all. Eventually, cattle were put in to the room but they all died. The roofless part of the house is still to be seen. The present occupier (a son of the former owner) would not use any fallen branches from around the well as firewood. This well and disused graveyard are shown on the Ordnance Map - Sheet 39 - Cork.

FROM KILMEADEN TO KILLEEDY
FOR ST. ITA'S FEAST DAY

It was the 15th January, a Monday and the Feast of St Ita. Many thoughts ran through the mind as I drove from Kilmeaden to Killeedy - from the County of Waterford to County Limerick. St. Ita had made a similar journey many centuries ago, and here I was making my own small pilgrimage to a celebration of her Feast Day, in a little Limerick village that had echoes of the Suirside village I know so well.

The people of Killeedy were expecting me, as I had been in touch with them over the preceding weeks about my proposed journey. All the way from Kilmeaden to Killeedy, the similarity of the placenames echoed and re-echoed in my mind. The origin of both names can, of course, be traced back to St. Ita. Kilmeaden in fact means Cill M'Ideán (the Church of My Little Ita).

Ita was an early Waterford saint, a Princess of the Déise who converted to Christianity. Her original church is said to have stood in the grounds of St. Mary's Church of Ireland in Kilmeaden. She also ministered to the people of West Waterford and later, she left the valley of the Blackwater and founded a monastery near Killeedy in Co. Limerick. Now, as I drew nearer and nearer to my destination, my mind flew back and forth between the place I had started from and the patch of Limerick soil to which Ita had also given her name.

I arrived in Killeedy just in time for the 11o'clock Mass in Raheenagh Church, which was filled to capacity. The porch was packed with young boys and I had to squeeze my way past them. Local schools are closed on the Feast of St. Ita, which is a parish holiday in Killeedy. A priest beckoned me up towards the front, near the altar, where a few seats still remained. It was an occasion of solemn importance and the Bishop of Limerick, Most Rev. Donal Murray arrived on the altar to celebrate Mass accompanied by seven priests. Bishop Murray spoke glowingly about St. Ita and the importance of her legacy. It was a beautiful Mass and there was a distinct feeling afterwards that people were the richer for it.

I visited the old graveyard, where tradition says Ita found her last resting place. It is a peaceful, well kept graveyard. People were walking around with their rosary beads in their hands. Locally this is known as making the rounds of the ruined Church of Killeedy. I asked one young couple if I could join in. The woman smiled and handed me a rosary beads. It was the first time I'd had one in my hands for many years and as we walked the boundary, her husband prayed aloud in Irish.

People knelt and prayed at St. Ita's grotto, set amid the old church ruins. A modern plaque marks the spot where St. Ita is said to be buried. There is a well, which was shown to me by a local priest, where people came with bottles to fill. I sipped the well-water from my cupped hands, just like we did in our youth, at home all those years ago on the farm in county Waterford.

That reflection reminded me that I seemed to be the only one from Waterford present among the large gathering of Limerick people and I found myself hoping that perhaps the following year we would be able to fill a bus or two with people from Ita's native place. Later, we adjourned to the local Community Hall, which was soon filled with people enjoying the fine meal provided by the women of the locality.

A solo musician named Michael Collins provided the music that brought everybody out onto the dance floor. Old and young enjoyed Irish dance music until the early hours of the morning, when the last echo of merriment died away across the grassy plains around the foot of Sliabh Luachra.

I had much to reflect on as I sat behind the wheel of my car on the road home next day. Kilmeaden, Killeedy; two places that shared the same saint. Would that not be a good reason to formally twin the two villages? I had travelled many miles, but it was truly a journey made up of more than mere miles. For me, it was a personal, spiritual pilgrimage. But it was also a profoundly communal event and there was a rich feeling that somehow we had all reached back across the centuries to commune with our own St. Ita.

Pictured above at St. Eannaigh's Well, Killineach, Abbeyfeale is Sr. Teresa Cotter 'who is 92 years of age.

Sr. Teresa spent her life in Fresno, California where she taught. She has already celebrated her Golden Jubilee. St. Ita also visited this well frequently on her way to the townland of Boolaveda in the Parish of Mouncollis where she grazed cattle and sheep. It was here that Ita first introduced her sister Eannaigh to the people of Limerick.

'There were no houses nearby, no raucous voices, no traffic, no din - just the murmur of a nearby stream, the twitter of birds and the lowing of animals in nearby fields. Killeenagh Well is not primarily a tribute to beautiful stonework, to the peace of the surrounding countryside or to the site of a well. It is primarily a tribute to the people of Abbeyfeale and to the durability of their faith which has survived to this day.'

Basket Making in Early Times

One day, Princess Ita was sitting in a shady grove and, as she rested, she watched the birds weaving their nests as instinct had taught them to do. They used the material which had been provided by God through nature and which was ideal for nesting. As she watched the birds at work, Ita learned how to weave twigs, stems, tough grass and rushes into baskets, one of the best and oldest of the Irish arts. Basket weaving is said to be the forerunner of cloth-making.

It was the mother of the home who usually made the baskets and this was what was used for the new-born baby's cradle. Baskets were used for almost all household chores. They were coated with gum to make them suitable for carrying water and some weavers were so skilled and could weave so tightly that they could carry water with only a coating of clay inside.

The first pottery vessels are said to have been made by smearing clay on baskets before baking them in a fire. Baskets were also used for cooking, having hot stones placed in them to bring water to the boil.

Sandals and very basic straw hats for protection from the sun were also made in this way, but the strongest of the baskets were kept for bringing firewood, fish, meat, clay and stones for household supplies.

Even in those early days, Celtic women had a sense of art and very often plaited hair was used as a decoration for these baskets or as a carrying handle. Most beautiful of all were the designs woven into the baskets representing the wonders of nature like the rainbow, flowers, trees, animals or mountains. This was one of the ways in which Celtic women expressed their feelings, their dreams as well as the traditions and ideals of their race.

ST BRENDAN
A CENTENARY TRIBUTE

One night that seemed as bright as day
Slieve Mish looked down on Trá Lí Bay
Whose silver waves washed Kerry's shore
And the year was AD five hundred and four.

And then and there was Brendan born
Whom neighbours greet at break of morn
Great deeds for him his friends foretell
'Ere he's baptised at Weather's well.

At six years old he's a foster child
Of Abbess Ita, wise and mild
With other infants whom she rears
Till they have come to reasonís years.

What love and care on him she showers
In his learning, praying and playing hours
Will shape his outlook and fill his mind
While his varied course the years unwind.

What songs there were, what smiles, what tears
At parting and perhaps what fears
The day that Bishop Erc came there
To take with him young Brendan fair.

With Erc he goes to green Ardfert
To live in prayer and till the earth,
To learn the psalms and sing them too
Ere rose the sun or dried the dew.

And so through work and resting rare
Through feasts, more oft through fasting spare
The child to youth and manhood grew
Then turned his thoughts to teachers new.

Some years he spends at Jarlath's school
Where he reads God's word and keeps the rule
And ere he goes he prophesies
Where his wheel will break will Jarlath rise.

With Enda's men in Aran soon
His every power he tries attune
To God's designs and so attain
To holiness whateíer the strain.

On Brandon mountain next he prays
Remote from man, on God his gaze
His thoughts uplifted by the sights
Revealed all round the mountain heights.

At night the stars above his head
Are silent as old Ireland's dead
In morning sun beneath his gaze
Half Munster lies in golden haze.

At noon from Aran to Kenmare
Entranced lie bays and islands fair
When the sun sinks down in pinks and greens
Its parting rays point west it seems.

When the sun went down in crimson flood
The world of legend stirred his blood
For after all it might be true
That west of the sun was a world new.

With the Land of Promise of the saints
The ancient tale his like acquaints
Its souls and beauty cast their spell
So he feels if he could find, 'twere well.

FIRST VOYAGE

He builds his boat, selects his crew
And to Corcaguiny bids adieu
Not a sail is set, not an oar is plied,
They plan to drift with God as guide.

The wind and currents bear them on,
Halts them the calm till their food is gone.
Thirsty and worn at last they land -
Thank God for drink and shore where they stand.

These landings were in Faroe Isles
When they had drifted countless miles.
One full of sheep now called Streymoy,
Vager the other where seabirds cry.

On a barren Island they contrived
To land but then the island dived.
(no need reject this fishy tale
Since we know it could have been a whale).

For forty days to land they try
But offshore winds their wish deny
Though fasting days to God they speak
And find at last a landing creek.

St. Ailbe's this, Madeira now
Where monks to greet them smile and bow
They Christmassed there and off again
To drift upon the Spanish Main.

Blown once again on island shores
This time to land on the Azores
Where water vile near killed the crew

In spite of all Brendan could do.
By wind and current west they float
Till a sea of weeds surrounds their boat ñ
Ten thousand weeds that cling like tape
Raise doubt and fear for their escape.

Escape they did to open sea
Where current and wind again play free -
The southwest wind and great Gulf Stream
Safe home bring Brendan and his team.

For five long years they had seen enough
To prove for ever they were tough -
These Irish monks severely trained
Could live when it scorched or snowed or rained.

They could live through terror, thirst or pain,
They could pray through all and hope again
They could bear exhaustion, lack of rest,
Godís will being clear, face any test.

Now Brendan's mind was not at peace,
But kept regretting without cease
Though he through wonders rare had gone
Still the Land of Promise called him on.

To Kileedy therefore he repairs
And tells his news, his problems airs
To Ita prudent and discreet
Of the winning ways and reason sweet.

Brendan
I can build a boat that needs no hides
A timber ship that will sail the tides
But I've sought so long and sought in vain
I shudder ere I try again.

Ita

Now Ita said with voice upraised
I'll design a boat that needs no hides
A timber ship to sail the tides
Youíve sought before, now try again.

Brendan

I've sought that Isle for five long years
In hope, despair, in peace and fears
I sought without a sail or oars
But never found the blessed shores

Ita

You did not use your oars or sails!
Oh child, you tell such funny tales!
As if God intends your mind unused
Or wished your hands from work excused.

Go forth again and you will find
The Blessed Isle. Just use your mind
And lore of stars to plot your course
With your hands on rudder, sails and oars.

Brendan

I find such sense in what you say
No course is left but to obey -
By the stars I'll steer forever west
And with sail and oar reached the Island Blessed.

SECOND VOYAGE

Another ship, another try
On plotted course by the stars on high
With sail and oar to beat the way
To the Blessed Isle so far away.

To Iceland first they navigate,
By Greenland, then across the Strait
To reach Newfoundland in the fall
Then coastwise south through many a squall.

Such in brief the way he came
To earn universal fame
'Twere easy now with ships and planes
But then a nightmare full of pains.

THE VOLCANO

At Iceland, terror gripped their frame
For rocky island belched in flame
And thunderous bellows underground

Said Brendan to them, 'Crewmen pray !
Live by your faith this woeful day
Be men ! your best ! and do it well
For, brethern, we're on the brink of hell'.

St. Brendan and his crew escape
Alive but yet in shattered shape
And so their nerves so badly strained
Present upon a rock enchained.

What seems a man who gives his name
As Judas of the Passion shame
And tells them of the nether woes
From which no prayer can bring repose.

THE HERMIT

They reach a rock like Skellig Mor
A narrow cove its open door
On its bare top lived Hermit Paul
Alone with God and God his all.

Since a monk of Patrick he had been
On this rock for ninety years between
Since Patrick told him here to pray
And leave his bones 'till Judgement Day.

On each third day an otter would
Bring twigs for fire and fish for food;
After thirty years the otter died
At a time when Paul a spring espied.

And at that spring his thirst he slaked,
Nor meat he killed nor bread he baked,
Nor hunger felt, nor his years curtailed
For 'twas sixty years since that spring he hailed.

When saying farewell to Brendan's crew
He gave them some of this rocky dew
On it they lived for forty days
Their hearts all joy like a harp that plays.

THE MONSTERS

By Greenland current west they go
Where the ocean still could wonders show
As when a beast with hungry throat
Bore down with power upon their boat

For from the west comes tearing past
Another monster cruel and fast;
In deadly conflict they engage
Turning white the sea with seething rage.

They flail and turn, lash and zoom
They bare their teeth, their nostrils fume
Savage their wounds as the red blood flows
Till the eastern fighter from weakness slows.

Fierce to the end the west one rears
And into pieces the east one tears
And westward bleeding then he goes
To the place from which at first he rose.

THE ICEBERG

Wonders all along the way
What's this on which the sunbeams play?
No doubt it's huge and wondrous too
So three day's sail brings it in full view.

A crystal palace here indeed
Beyond the size of human need
A marvel this from God's own hand
Perhaps the gate to the Promised Land.

For four full days they stay longside
This magic castle on the tide
And all the time they fast and pray
For it may be voyagers' landing day.

They marvel at the soaring spire
The dazzling roof, the dream entire,
The shining columns dipped in waves
The arches vast as churchesí naves.

Through one of these at last they go
And find all inside with light aglow
A light that shines through roof and floor
For fathoms down beneath their oar.

They bid goodbye to the lustrous pile
Sad 'twas not the Blessed Isle
Having steered through thick Newfoundland dark
On sunny seas they soon embark.

The sea gave up its mystery
As to its depths the eye could see
Huge shoals of fish in vivid hue,
The big, the small, the monsters too.

All panickstruck the crewmen feel
And now to Brendan they appeal
"Dear Father Prior, you'll be our doom
These monsters here will be our tomb".

"Please Father Prior, please lower your tone
For all our sakes and for your own.
If fish can hear, you'll draw them near
They'll gulp us down, that's what we fear."

"You need not fear, take heart! be brave!
For Christ rules too beneath the wave!"
Then raised his tone till Mass was said
At which the monsters turned and fled.

WESTERN LANDFALL

Bahama shores soon meet their gaze
Where herbs and fruit call out their praise,
Where rest revives the little band
Ere off once more for the Promised Land.

Just one stage more and that the best
For now they reach the Island Blest
Behold, the land in legend famed
Shines there in light that never waned.

A spacious land of many trees
O'er grass that crooned in gentle breeze;
Bright flamed the leaves in autumn hue.
Green, yellow, brown, bright scarlet too.

No briars, no blight to hurt their sight,
No fog, no cloud -to dim the light ñ
Delicious fruits to please the tongue
With enchanting scents around them hung.

For forty days they travel round
No limit to this land they found
Till they reach a river deep and wide
Which guards from them the other side.

My theme is peace to men of peace
My theme is joy and joys increase
To men of God who will obey
When He says 'Home! and in homeland stay".

"For many moons you sought our land
But God allowed you understand
The awful seas that lie between
Our golden-west and Ireland ever green."

"Return now, return straight, you feel that breeze
'Twill take you home across the seas
Bid long farewell to Isle of Blessed
Return home to peace and rest."

"Take all you wish - gems, fruit and plants
At home they will your tale enhance
And thank your God you came and saw
And left before I had to draw".
(he shows his bow and arrows)

"But when your land lacks peace and food
You'll find us in another mood;
Your children weak can stand no more
Then bid them seek our generous shore.

RETURN

The southwest wind and strong Gulf Stream
Bear home the Captain and his team
The welcome o'er, the tale retold
On Irish minds takes firm hold.

Disciples came from far and near
The pious leader's words to hear
God's wonders gave his sermons scope
God's providence inspired new hope.

His word and rule lead minds to soar
In Kilmalkeader and Blasketmore
In old Ardfert his bell rang out
Drawing pious souls from all about.

Though ageing now his heart was young
His one idea - God's praise he sung
So away he goes to spread the news
And point the path that men should choose.

What now is Coney Isand saw
Him mould his men with firm law
Connaught fell beneath his spell
And Innis Gloria heard his bell.

At Inchiguin on Corrib Lake
His monks their cells and chapel make
To Annaghdown where the skylark sings
His sister Briga's nuns he brings.

In Scottish isles we find his name
In Briton lands we glimpse his fame
And scholars find his echoes still
On Grecian isles and Sion's hill.

CLONFERT

Old and worn now he is
And looks on time and eternity
He's lost in verve and youthful drive,
He plans to make his work survive.

He longs to teach what he had learned
He must share out his wisdom earned
In fast and prayer, voyage, march and book
Of pleasing God in voice and look.

The praise of God, the One in Three,
His Power's expanse past land and sea,
His mercy to the man of trust -
To teach all this was Brendan's must.

Through worlds of space and leagues of time
How to shine God's laws and truths sublime?
His answer was the Clonfert School
Where thousands lived and prayed the rule.

For twenty years this school he steers
As it grew in strength with passing years
It thrived a thousand years in all
And 'tis there his dust awaits the Call.

DEATH

At Annaghdown when ninety four
The sailor feels he's nearing shore,
He feels perhaps a sing-song hush

A Chill? Perhaps a thirst of love
Told him his place was soon above
And he said "The Lord is calling me
Pray! Pray! Pray for me!"

Then Briga said, "Why should you fear?
You've lived a saintly life while here."
"I fear the dark-lone-way
I fear the Word the Judge will say."

"We have more cause to fear and grieve
Please to us all your blessing give."
"My blessing now I will bestow
If to Clonfert my funeral go."

(They bow, he blesses them)

"To the chapel now for journey's end. (He kneels)
To God my spirit I commend".
(he prays in silence and dies).

THE END

Songs of Our Land
by Frances Brown

Songs of our land, ye are with us for ever,
The power and the splendor of thrones pass away;
But yours is the might of some far flowing river.
Through Summer's bright roses or Autumn's decay.

Ye treasure each voice of the swift passing ages,
And truth which time writeth on leaves or on sand;
Ye bring us the thoughts of poets and sages,
And keep them among us, old songs of our land.

The bards may go down to the place of their slumbers,
The lyre of the charmer be hushed in the grave,
But far in the future the power of their numbers
Shall kindle the hearts of our faithful and brave,

It will waken an echo in souls deep and lonely,
Like voices of reeds by the summer breeze fanned;
It will call up a spirit for freedom, when only
Her breathings are heard in the songs of our land.

For they keep a record of those, the true-hearted,
Who fell with the cause they had vowed to maintain;
They show us bright shadows of glory departed,
Of love that grew cold and hope that was vain.

The page may be lost and the pen long forsaken,
And weeds may grow wild o'er the brave heart and hand;
But ye are still left when all else hath been taken,
Like streams in the desert, sweet songs of our land.

Songs of our land, ye have followed the stranger,
With power over ocean and desert afar,
Ye have gone with our wanderers through distance and danger,
And gladdened their path like a homeguiding star.

With the breath of our mountains in summers long vanished,
And visions that passed like a wave from the sand,
With hope for their country and joy from her banished.
Ye come to us ever, sweet songs of our land.

The spring time may come with the song of our glory,
To bid the green heart of the forest rejoice,
But the pine of the mountain though blasted and hoary,
And the rock in the desert, can send forth a voice,

It was thus in their triumph for deep desolations,
While ocean waves roll or the mountains shall stand,
Still hearts that are bravest and best of the nations,
Shall glory and live in the songs of our land.

THE FOURPENNY HOP

Going to Killeady was great fun,
Some would cycle and some would run.
More did trot, and others did walk,
All together, they would sing and talk.

Parking the bike, it cost three pence,
But some would park, against the old fence,
The bicycle clips were put in your pocket,
Then into the dance, like a pure rocket.

Going into the hall, the girls were free,
It was four pence for the boys, and they got no tea.
They danced and danced under the oil light,
And enjoyed themselves for the rest of the night.

When the dance was over, the fun began,
Chris in the loft, what a lovely quiet man.
He minded the bikes, and was waiting around,
For the courting couples, who had gone to ground.

One by one they came back for their bike,
It looked as if they were stuck in a dyke.
Chris was waiting, I can't tell you what he said,
All he wanted was to get home to bed.

In those times, it was harmless fun,
Whether you had to cycle, or to run,
Going to Killeady was mighty crack,
And one thing for sure, you always went back.

John L. O'Sullivan

Appendix 2
The Celtic People and Culture

The Celtic people came from Europe and were known as wanderers who wanted to explore the world. Their culture marked them out as special people. They had no written language but loved to talk and were great storytellers and singers. They showed great courage and bravery in battle and were never frightened on land or at sea as they drifted wherever their boats took them. The Celts were also a people gifted in the skills of making weapons of war and their leaders were colourfully and suitably dressed when going into battle. When beaten and downtrodden, they would gather together to sing their fighting songs and then return to the battlefield to fight on.

Historically, the Celtic tradition has survived better in Ireland than among any other nation. Modern Irish Gaelic is a close descendant of the ancient Celtic language and is still spoken in some areas. These traditions and ballads were sung by young Irish men and women at Mass in times of emigration and when seeking work after the great famine in 1810. These songs are addressed to the legendary heroes of Ireland to conjure up a distant golden age, a typical use of their myth. These emigrants themselves have become legendary with their songs.

*   *   *   *   *

The finest of the many stories connected to the life and miracles of St. Ita, have not been written down. Records of the period ranging over the one to four centuries after her death and also of her journeys through Munster must have been lost, yet the folklore lived on. Not only was Ita known as the Mary of Munster, as it was said she fostered the child Jesus, she was also known as the Brigid of Munster and the Bright Sun of Munster. Another title by which she was also known was Mother of Vocations, as she sent priests and messengers all over the world to bring the Christian faith and the Word of God to many. Some caution must be applied to the material in all medieval manuscripts.

The content in the foregoing pages is drawn from sources provided by the people of various parishes, supported by documented tradition, folklore researched by school children, as well as by school master historian and priest, Bruno Donoghue and confirmed by Ita Vaughan O'Neill, Gortroe, Youghal, Co. Cork. We can truly consider these stories by the people of Munster to their beloved St. Ita.

It is said that Ita negotiated with Pope John II (533 - 535) and the Holy Father, throughout his reign, always wanted news of the holy Celtic Saint Ita and he used her elevation to sainthood to demonstrate her feminine equality with men.

Many miracles of extraordinary character are attributed to the Holy Virgin Ita, in such acts as restoring the sick and infirm to health and even on several occasions, raising the dead to life. She is said to have had a knowledge of transgressions which were thought to have been secret, known only to God. Because from infancy she was accustomed to meditating on Divine matters, she had been favoured with supernatural powers and if these were lacking in chronicles of her time, the chroniclers paid the penalty of seeing their books cast aside as stale and unproductive.

It is through this love of the sensational among simple souls that the real and truthful record of martyrs ordeals survived. We cannot say whether these stories which have been distorted or embellished, are true or not. Little is known or written about St. Ita through Munster, though it is known that she travelled the counties of this province, as there are many stories handed down through generations of folklore about her, especially in places called Kilmeedy, Killeedy and Kilmeaden, which are called after St. Ita.

Ita travelled like Joan of Arc. She fought the Druids and freed poor people in many places in Munster and Leinster.

Acknowledgements

The author acknowledges with deep thanks and appreciation the co-operation he received from the many people with whom he spoke in the course of his research and also the hospitality he enjoyed in the various locations in all the Counties of Munster as well as parts of Leinster particularly Malahide, Co. Dublin and Kilmeade, Co. Kildare where he went in search of information about St. Ita.

He extends a special thanks to:

James Guiry
Sr. M Íde ni Riain RSCJ
Edward Leahy

Members of the Clergy who gave me advice and guidance

The Kerry Co. Librarian and members of Tralee Library Staff, particularly Eamonn Fitzgerald, Heritage and Local History Section.

Other authors who gave me permission to quote from their work

Tom and Carmel Keith for their technical assistance

**and particular thanks
to my wife Ann,
sister in law, Mary Dunphy
and the members of my family for their constant support
and assistance through
what was a lengthy and demanding project.**